BLIZZARD RANGE

Center Point
Large Print

**This Large Print Book carries the
Seal of Approval of N.A.V.H.**

TODHUNTER BALLARD

BLIZZARD RANGE

CENTER POINT PUBLISHING

THORNDIKE, MAINE

This Center Point Large Print edition
is published in the year 2003 by arrangement with
Golden West Literary Agency.

The text of this Large Print edition is unabridged. In other
aspects, this book may vary from the original edition. Printed in
Thailand. Set in 16-point Times New Roman type by
Bill Coskrey and Gary Socquet.

ISBN 1-58547-316-2

Library of Congress Cataloging-in-Publication Data.

Ballard, Todhunter, 1903-
    Blizzard range / Todhunter Ballard.--Center Point large print ed.
        p. cm.
    ISBN 1-58547-316-2 (lib. bdg. : alk. paper)
    1. Large type books. I. Title.

PS3503.A5575B55 2003

2003040958

CHAPTER 1

SNOW LAY like a rumpled, rippled blanket upon the land, a cover which glistened in the sun, looking deceptively harmless, clean and protective, turning the twisting hills into mounds of a baker's art, like a dessert capped by a white meringue.

It had snowed again that morning, the fifth time in as many days, and the new fall had buried the soiled patches and blanketed the pines and the bare aspen with its sticky flakes until some branches had swelled to twice their normal size.

The sun dropped now, nearing the icy crest of the Goldanions, drawing its last flaming path across the curving road as Tolliver's horse breasted the fresh drifts to come down the short grade and turn into Benton's main thoroughfare.

As if recognizing the end of its struggle, the animal quickened its pace, aiming for Parkingstead's Livery, and once inside the hay-floored runway heaved a deep-felt sigh and let its head hang low in quiet, restful content.

Tolliver stepped down. He was a big man with an under-frame of heavy bone which knew very little flesh, a tall man, his dark face turned red by the rawness of the weather, his blue eyes seeming icy against the red, as if they had picked up a reflection from the countryside through which he had been riding.

Parkingstead came from the office, balancing himself on the peg which he had worn ever since Gettysburg, and smiled his welcome through his bushy beard.

"A dinger." He spat under the fore-feet of Tolliver's horse. "A week of snow, with sunshine in between. I've never seen the like in thirty years."

Tolliver nodded abstractedly. "She's three feet deep on the level, but most of the stock is in the home pasture now. If the hay holds out we'll see no trouble."

The livery man spat again. "You staying in?"

"I think so," Tolliver said. "Martha's at the hotel, and we could both use a little fun. Big crowd expected for the dance?"

"If it don't snow." The old man cackled and led the horse away.

Tolliver stared after him for a moment, then turned and came back out onto Benton's main street and looked at the three block length of the town.

Very little traffic had passed since three, when the snow had stopped its fall, and the white expanse of the road was nearly unmarked.

The houses, under the heavy loads on their roofs, looked smaller than usual, like sections of a miniature buried in a sea of sifted flour.

The wind struck him, the first evening down-draft, bursting out of the pass seventy miles away and kicking snow in little swirling eddies which chased each other between the buildings like playful dust devils on a hot August afternoon.

But it was no August afternoon. The thermometer in front of Bailey's store said fourteen above zero. He read it, his big-knuckled hands thrust into the slash pockets of his sheeplined coat, and stomped on to the Star along the slatted walk.

Winter doors replaced the batwing, and he fumbled twice with the heavy lock before he got it open and came into the overheated interior, rich with the smell of whiskey and wood smoke from the big wood stove, and human bodies.

Curly, the bartender, was just lighting the center lamp, and four men played cards at a rear table. Otherwise the big room was unoccupied.

Tolliver moved to the bar and without a word Curly set out a glass, lifted a kettle from the stove, added sugar to the whiskey and then poured in the steaming water.

"Warms a man," he said, noticing the small particles of ice which still clung to Tolliver's eyebrows. "She's a dinger."

A dinger, thought Tolliver, and sipped the warming drink. The town's word for it. He'd heard the phrase a dozen times this last week. He didn't know who had started it, but in a small, shut-in community like the valley words and phrases made their rounds, regularly.

He finished the drink and stood before the stove, loosening his coat. One button hung by a single thread, and he stared at it in passing resentment. To his mind it represented his daily life.

A bachelor. A man in a saddle. A man without a wife to sew on his buttons and cook his meals. He tugged out of the coat and hung it on a wall peg, and then moved over to the card table and stood watching in silence until the hand was played.

From old acquaintance he knew the deadly seriousness with which these men took their cards, and he would no more have interrupted than he would have interfered in a private quarrel between a man and his wife.

When the hand had been played and the small pile of chips won by Zeeman, the marshal, he pulled out an empty chair and sank into it.

"Do you amateurs want an experienced hand in the game, or are you afraid of real ability?"

Dorchester, who ran both the saloon and the game, answered by pushing a stack of chips in his direction. He pretended to count them, carefully, murmuring,

"My mother always said never to trust a gambling man." He found the chips correct and rolled a twenty dollar gold piece across the board.

Dorchester's narrow face had a blank look. "Sometime your joke will backfire, Owen."

Owen Tolliver grinned at him. "We're all getting cabin fever," he said. "When Hal Dorchester can't laugh at my jokes it's time for winter to be past."

Bryan Hall said, "Are we playing poker or are we insulting each other?" It was his deal and he gathered up the cards. "A quarter, gentlemen, so we have something to play for."

Tolliver said, "There speaks a banker. Bryan can't even afford to deal a hand unless he sees his interest on the table."

Hall did not have as careful control of his face muscles as Dorchester did. He said, "For one, Owen, I have never found you amusing."

"I know you haven't," said Tolliver, "which is bad, because you have always amused me, ever since we were in school."

The banker's flush deepened, but he took his quick anger out in slapping the cards down upon the table.

Pop Rand, who had run the blacksmith shop since any of them could remember, said mildly, "You've been riding alone too much, Owen. A man out of a sleet storm usually has a chip on his shoulder."

Owen looked at him. He looked at the other men around the table. He had known them all his life and he thought, I'll never learn. There isn't a spark of humor in the whole group. There's hardly a bit of humor in the town, or in the valley around it. I make my little jokes and they fall flat, and I feel like the damn fool I am.

He said, "Sorry, Pop," and did not mean it. He had been in the saddle since long before sunup, and he had ridden hard and was tired. He had looked forward to some companionship after the weary, snow-covered miles, and he found little here.

He thought of Martha waiting for him at the hotel. Martha had little use for humor either. Martha was practical. It always puzzled him how anyone so beautiful could be so practical.

Well, Martha was Martha, just as he was Owen Tolliver. People are what they are, as old Joe John had been wont to say. You can't change them, and you

9

can't kill them all, so you just have to make up your mind to live with them.

Tolliver could remember the old man saying it. He had said it more than once, whenever one of his neighbors had particularly annoyed him. Old Joe John had had a sense of humor, and he had needed it, all through the long lean years when he had first come into the valley.

Tolliver missed him as he might have missed the father he had never known. And he supposed that the whole valley missed the old man. Certainly Martha missed her father, but in some ways, he knew, he had been closer to Joe John than even she had.

He lost the pot, and the next, and realized that he was not concentrating on the game. He heard Bryan Hall ask him how the cattle were weathering the storm and he shrugged.

"We're in pretty good shape," he admitted. "Of course, we've had three days of tough riding, but this caught us with the cows still up on the benches and we had to get them down. A cow brute isn't like a horse or a jack. They'll scratch down through five feet of snow if there's a blade of grass anywhere. A cow won't. A cow will stand there and starve."

No one said anything. They might be townspeople, but this was a cattle country and every dollar in it came from stock.

He yawned. "Maybe we'll have an early spring." The heat from the stove and from the warm drink Curly had given him were making him sleepy. He wondered what

Martha would say if he tried to beg off from the dance. Martha would be very angry. Martha loved to dance.

When he lost the last of his chips he thrust back his chair and rose. "I'm a plumb fool," he told them. "I shorten my life riding out in all kinds of weather to make an honest dollar, then I bring it in here and let you chair warming thieves take it away."

None of them grinned and he turned toward the door, pausing at the bar to say, "Let me have one more, Curly. I always heard alcohol wouldn't freeze, and in this weather a man has to do something to keep from turning into a cake of ice."

The bartender served him. Then he thought of something. "Forgot to tell you. There was a breed in here this afternoon, looking for you."

Tolliver had little interest. "What'd he want?"

"Wouldn't know. Last I saw of him he was heading for Perkins' restaurant. Probably wanted a job riding grub line."

Tolliver nodded and slipped into his coat. As he came out of the saloon the wind struck him with icy force, knocking him awake. He stood for a moment, his back pressed to the wall in an effort to escape the full blast of the air.

Lights showed now in almost every building, casting their yellow paths across the blowing snow. It was colder. He could tell by the way the snow squealed beneath his boots as he stepped, but despite the snow and the cold the town was gradually coming to life. As he stood there three rigs passed, heading for the livery, and four horsemen from the north rim galloped by. It took more than freezing weather to keep the valley away from a dance.

He started toward the hotel, but seeing Grace Perkins through the cloudy window of the restaurant he hesitated for a moment and then turned in.

There were only half a dozen diners in the place since it was yet early, and she came forward as soon as he stepped through the door.

"Owen." There was a welcome warmth in her tone. "I wondered if you were buried in a snow bank under the south rim."

He grinned at her, feeling the rich pleasure that he always experienced in her presence. "Came to speak for a couple of dances tonight."

She was tall for a woman, and dark where Martha was fair, and there was a certain quiet dignity about her which he had found restraining until he had noticed the glint of humor hidden in her grey eyes.

She was not a valley girl. Her family had moved in less than three years before, and he had never known her well until the preceding summer, when her engagement to Bryan Hall had been announced at the Fourth of July celebration.

He studied her now, remembering Hall as he had seen him at the card table a few minutes before, and wondered again at this coming alliance.

There was something pompous about Hall, despite his youth, a stuffiness which Owen Tolliver had always found irritating, an air of importance which had grown steadily as Hall progressed at the bank.

Twenty years from now Hall would be a little fat, his hair a little thin, his ego a little more developed. It was a distressing picture, and Owen Tolliver knew a feeling of surprise that this girl before him, who was so clever about most things, should fail to see the weaknesses of the man she was to marry.

She said now, "Shouldn't you speak to Bryan? Isn't that the way things are done, dances traded?"

He grinned. "You know, I doubt that even the thought of a chance to dance with Martha would prompt Bryan to do me a favor."

Her eyes clouded a little. "You don't like him, do you, Owen?"

He was tempted in the moment to tell her what he really thought, but he curbed the impulse, saying instead, "Bryan and I have been fighting ever since we were kids."

She felt the evasion, but she let it pass, and her well formed lips were touched by a small smile. "I know that Bryan was interested in Martha before I came. I think some of the old feeling lingers, that that's the reason you and he are not close friends."

He knew a sudden, quick sympathy for her. It was no secret in the valley that Bryan Hall had once hoped to marry Martha, and at one time Martha had encouraged his attention. She was a woman who needed admiration, and with her beauty she had attracted men from the whole corner of the Territory. But when the showdown came it was Tolliver she had chosen.

The choice had surprised Owen as much as anyone, and he had never been certain in his own mind that Joe John had not influenced it. Certainly Joe John had been pleased when he learned that his daughter had decided on Tolliver.

"You're getting a bargain," he'd told the younger man. "She's got a level head on her shoulders, like her mother had." He sighed as he said it, and Tolliver could not tell whether the sigh was evoked by the memory of his dead wife or by his pleasure that his daughter was to marry.

Owen said now, "Don't make the mistake of thinking Bryan and I are enemies. It's just that we don't see things eye to eye. It's my fault, mostly." He said this honestly because it was true. "I never let him alone. I always made a little fun of him."

Her smile deepened. "He hasn't too much sense of humor, has he? But do me a favor, Owen. Try to be a little more friendly toward him. In a perverse sort of way he admires you. You are in fact about the only man in the whole valley for whom he has much respect, even though it shows as a form of jealousy because you can do so many things well which he would like to do and can't. It could be turned into friendship if you tried."

Because he liked her genuinely he said, "I'll try. I'll see you at the dance." He turned, and had the door half open when she stopped him.

"Owen, I forgot, there's an Indian here to see you. He came in this afternoon, and he was so cold I let him stay in the storeroom. Come on." She led the way toward the kitchen.

CHAPTER 2

JOHNNY SHORT BEAR had been asleep, his head on a sack of potatoes, his moccasined feet out-stretched across the bare floor. He came awake as the storeroom door was pushed open, and seeing Tolliver standing above him he rose quickly to his feet.

He was nineteen, and he was short even for one of his race, but he was also strong, and he had made the trip through the snow-filled pass from the reservation in three days and two nights.

He stood now, trying to steady himself, his thin face showing his weariness and hunger, his dark eyes looking up at the bigger man.

"You Tolliver?"

Owen nodded.

"I came to find Joe John."

"He's dead," Tolliver told him. "He died last September."

Short Bear could speak as good English as anyone, but he was not a person to waste words. "I know. They tell me at ranch. Man called Shorty, say to see you. Say you be here today."

Tolliver nodded. He asked suddenly, "When did you eat last?"

The Indian made a gesture with a dirty hand. "Two, three days ago."

Behind Tolliver came an exclamation, then Grace's voice. "Owen, it never occurred to me that he was hungry. Bring him into the kitchen."

There was a dignity about the Indian that was almost painful to see. "No money."

Owen said, "When your people come to the ranch they don't expect to pay for food. It is the same here. This is a friend."

The Indian inspected Grace Perkins as if she were a curiosity from another world, then he nodded and without a word of thanks followed Tolliver to the kitchen table where Grace was already setting out a heaping plate of meat and potatoes and beans.

He ate silently, wolfishly, and they stood waiting until he had finished.

Finally he looked up, saying simply, "All my people starve. Joe John say when we need help, we come to him."

Tolliver nodded. Grace was looking at him and he read the question in her eyes. He said softly, "When Joe John came into this valley first, nearly fifty years ago, he made a deal with the Indians. This was all Indian country then, and a white man stood no chance if they were against him. But this tribe was friendly. They helped Joe John and he helped them, and later, when they were put on the reservation, he fought their battles with the Army and with the Indian agent. He always said that this valley was originally theirs, that he and the rest of us were only squatters, and that anything they wanted they could have."

Short Bear listened to this with no change of expression. He repeated now, "My people starve. There is no beef."

Tolliver was used to dealing with Indians. He said, "Why do they starve?"

"The agent is a fool."

This was an opinion which Tolliver shared. Edward Lord, who had been resident agent at the reservation for the last two years, was a well-meaning but blundering man.

"What has he done now?"

"Last fall he did not buy cattle for us in this valley."

This Tolliver knew also. It was the first time in the twenty years since the Indians had been put on the reservation that their winter supply of beef had not been purchased in the valley.

"What did he do?"

"He went over the mountains to the north and bought beef cheaper. But up there they waited too long. The snow was ten feet deep when they tried to drive over the crest."

"When was this?"

"Four weeks ago."

"And what has Lord done since?"

"Talk. He said that the snows came early, that there would be a thaw. He was wrong. There is more snow, and we are hungry. Then he sent for my grandfather, the Chief, and said we should come to Joe John, that Joe John would help us. He said to tell Joe John he will pay the price as asked. The money is ready, waiting."

Grace spoke without thinking. "But it's seventy miles to the pass, and there must be six or seven feet of snow up there."

The Indian did not turn to look at her. It was as if he realized that the decision rested with the big man before him.

Tolliver said slowly, "You came down through the pass, on snow shoes?"

Short Bear nodded.

"Can cattle get through?"

Short Bear's shoulder movement was expressive, but he said, "Joe John would get through."

Owen Tolliver agreed. Joe John hadn't been very big, he had never weighed over a hundred and twenty pounds in his life, but Joe John had been tough. Very few things had stopped him.

"You rest," said Owen. "We'll start the drive in the morning. You'd better get word to the reservation, and we could use some help in the pass."

"My people will be there," Short Bear said, and Owen turned to Grace.

"He can sleep in your storeroom, if I get a blanket for him?"

"But of course."

Short Bear moved away. Now that he was full, he wanted sleep. Grace followed Tolliver to the door, saying worriedly, "What are you going to do?"

He looked back in quick surprise. "Why, get some cattle up there. What else? You can't let four hundred people starve."

She was staring at him. "The way you say it, it sounds easy."

He knew a sudden impatience. "Nothing much in life is easy."

"But why is it your responsibility?"

He was silent for an instant, his mind running back over the years. "You didn't know Joe John very well, did you?"

"I've seen him," she said. "A funny little man with stringy whiskers."

He said soberly, "He was about the biggest man this country ever saw, or any country for that matter. He always figured that he owed those Indians the biggest debt a man can owe, and he paid his debts."

"You loved him, didn't you?"

He was startled. The word love in connection with Joe John Martel struck a strange note. Joe John had spent most of his life on the range. He had been an untidy, unprepossessing man who smelled of horses and cheap tobacco. Love . . . yes, he realized that he had loved the old man in a way he would never love anyone else.

"I guess so," he said. "Anyhow, I'll have to do what he would, if he were still here. I'll have to get those cows through." He turned then and opening the door, went out into the chill, windy night. He did not look back. He did not know that Grace stood at the steamy window watching him until he turned in at the hotel, and that there was a soft look in her eyes, a look that had not been there for anyone before.

CHAPTER 3

MARTHA MARTEL had moved into the hotel after her father's death. She had explained it quite logically to Tolliver, and while he had not been too pleased with the arrangement, he saw the validity of her position.

"I'd have to get a woman to stay with me at the ranch," she'd told him. "And you know how difficult it is to find anyone who will stay in the country during the winter."

He'd nodded.

"I couldn't stay out there with just you and the crew. It wouldn't look right to the country."

Owen Tolliver was not one who cared much what the country thought, but he supposed it was different with women. "We could," he suggested, "get married. Then it would be all right."

She was horrified. He could tell by her expression. "With father hardly buried? We'll have to wait at least six months."

They were waiting six months. Owen Tolliver seldom argued with Martha, and he realized that she liked living in town much better than she did at the ranch during the winter months. Nor could he blame her for this. Life could be terribly monotonous when you were separated from town by fifteen snowy miles.

She was waiting for him in the lobby, and her mouth and eyes showed her displeasure at his lateness, but he hardly noticed. It always gave him a lift to see her. She was so pretty. That was the thought he had always had, ever since she began to grow up.

She was the child of Joe John's old age, for her father had not married until he was nearing fifty, and it seemed incredible to everyone, including Tolliver, that Joe John could have sired such a handsome girl.

She was, Tolliver realized, a little spoiled, but that was natural enough since her mother had died when she was only twelve and from that day the old man had granted practically her every wish.

She said now in a dissatisfied voice, "I saw you ride in over an hour ago. Was it necessary to stop at the Star?"

His mouth quirked and his eyes lighted with their ready humor. "Not necessary, but darn warming. It was cold on the south benches this afternoon."

She forgot her annoyance in her quick interest. "Did you get them all down safely?"

He nodded. "The last of them yesterday. I rode back this morning to see if a stray was holed up in the box canyons. No sign."

"Have we enough hay?"

Again he nodded. "Unless this lasts forever I think we are all right." He did not remind her that he had had to fight both her and Joe John to put up the last two stacks. They had thought he was crazy to want so much.

She sighed a little then. "I've missed you, Owen. It isn't too much fun in town without you."

He almost told her that it wasn't much fun at the ranch either, with neither her nor Joe John there. He was living alone in the big house, the three man crew in the bunk shed. But he let it pass. He had never been entirely easy with her since the night he had realized she was no longer a child, when they had been coming home from a dance in the old buggy, and suddenly she was in his arms, kissing him.

That hadn't been so long ago, only four years, but often during the last months it had seemed a lifetime, and he said suddenly,

"Let's get married, Martha. Let's don't put it off any longer." He didn't know why he spoke. He'd had no idea of saying this when he'd entered the hotel. But somehow tonight he felt an unease, an impending foreboding which he could not explain.

He felt that it would be better for both of them if they got married now, this minute. He didn't know what was the matter with him. Maybe it was the Indian, and the thought of the four hundred people starving, up beyond the pass, people he had to help because a dead man had made a promise long ago.

She softened a little. She was a person who could always be reached through her vanity. And the knowledge that he wanted her, needed her, touched some hidden spring and brought her sharply alive.

"Owen, we can't. It's too soon. In February, like we planned." She glanced quickly about the long lobby to be certain they were alone, then she came against him, his big arms opening automatically to receive her, her young body warm and hard, yet yielding against him as he bent to kiss her.

They stood for a long moment, locked in a tight embrace and she said softly against his lips, "Darling, I get so very tired of waiting also."

He let her go then. His pulse was faster and some of the vague trouble in him had flowed away. Looking down at her small face, at the blue eyes which seemed a little too big for the rest of her, he could not help thinking how very lucky he was.

He realized suddenly that he had always been lucky. As a boy he had not thought so, since his father had been killed in a stage accident before he could remember, and his mother after struggling for years to support him had died when he was fourteen.

But then Joe John had taken him to the ranch, and he had been there ever since, first as a hand and afterward as the foreman.

As long as the old man had lived the title had been one of honor more than authority, since they never had more than three or four at most in the crew. But it had been an excuse to pay him a few additional dollars a month, an excuse for him to live at the big house.

Joe John had fathered him, and trained him, and now he was to marry Joe John's daughter and have the ranch besides. What more luck could a man have?

Martha was saying, "If we're going to be at the dance on time you'd better get cleaned up, and eat."

He nodded. He moved around the high hotel desk, and selected one of the keys from the rack and climbed the stairs, carrying his small war roll, its center holding a clean shirt. Not until he had stripped to the waist and was washing himself in the cold water from the pitcher did he remember that he had not mentioned the Indian to Martha.

He told her about it at supper. He let a little anger creep into his voice when he spoke of Edward Lord, the Indian agent.

"The man's a damn fool," he said. "He has no more business in this country than I would have in Washington. Why can't the Indian bureau pick people who understand Indians, who know what conditions are out here, and how to meet them? If they'd spend more money on getting good men they wouldn't have to spend so much on the army to keep the Indians from running off the reservations."

She smiled at him. "I love you when you get so worked up, Owen. You sound like a politician running for office."

He grinned, but the grin was weak. "Damnit, I'm right. So now because Lord tried to get foxy last fall and buy cheap beef up north, I have to put eight hundred cows through that pass if it kills me."

She said soberly, "Why do you have to do it?"

He looked at her sharply. "Why don't I? They didn't know Joe John was dead. They sent to him for help. You know damn well that if he were alive he'd get those cows to them if he had to carry every one on his back."

Her mouth thinned out a little. "That was Joe John.

He felt that his agreement with the old chief held, but how long must it go on? Over the years he returned to them a hundredfold everything they did for him."

Owen was silent.

She softened. "I know how you felt about Joe John. I know because I feel the same way. He was a great man, but Joe John never asked anyone to carry his burdens, he carried them for himself."

"He's dead. That leaves me to carry this burden."

"Why you?"

He shrugged, and she let a hint of annoyance show in her voice. "I know you are stubborn, Owen, and I honor you for it. I wouldn't give much for a man who wouldn't stand up for what he believes even if a woman asked him not to, but use a little reason too."

"Are you asking me not to go?"

She said, "I'm not asking, but think about it for a minute. You can't drive cattle that far through all this snow. They'd all die. And if you could, where would you get the cows?"

He hesitated for the barest instant. "At the dance tonight. Nearly everyone in the valley will be there. I'll apportion the herd among them."

She dropped her head, hiding her quick, distant smile. "Of course, if they will all agree."

Again he looked at her in surprise. "Why not? There isn't a man in the whole valley who doesn't owe his start to your father. And they know how he felt about the Indians. It was no secret."

He repeated the words an hour later at the dance. He

stepped out onto the floor after the second square, and motioned the three piece orchestra into silence. The room was well filled. The chairs lined along the wall held the elder members of the community. The rear room was filled with sleeping children.

Outside the temperature had dropped to zero, but inside the big lighted room it was cheerful with warmth.

He had their attention, and he stood for an instant, feeling a little uncertain as he looked at their faces. These were the people he had been raised with, who had known him all his life. It would have been far easier to talk to strangers.

He said:

"Something has happened which we've all got to do something about. The Indians over on the reservation are starving. The damn fool agent tried to buy northern cattle for them because he could buy cheaper than he could here. The men he bought from waited too long to start their drive. They can't get through, so, it's up to us."

He felt them stir under the thought. He waited, knowing that these people needed time, that their decisions were slowly taken.

Bryan Hall was standing directly in front of him, with Grace Perkins at his side. Before Tolliver was ready to speak again, he raised his voice. "And why should we do anything about it? The agent made the mistake, not buying our cattle. So now you want every man in the valley to throw away part of his herd, sending them through the pass? What happens when they don't get through? Will the agent pay for the beef you lose in the snow?"

Owen managed to mask his quick surprise. For an instant he assumed that Grace had told the banker about the Indians, and then he realized that Hall had said he was asking every man in the valley to furnish part of the herd. Hall might have guessed it, of course, but he thought not. He had mentioned his intention to Martha alone, and he knew with sudden sure certainty that she had talked to Hall.

He thought, she's opposed to the idea, but rather than stand against me directly, she's already been enlisting help to block me, behind my back. He was abruptly angry. One thing which he expected of life was loyalty. It was the code under which he had grown up. You stood with your own, with your ranch and your crew and your community.

But he kept the anger out of his voice, saying pleasantly, "You're jumping at conclusions, Bryan, and you are one of the few men in this room who will not be affected. You own no cattle."

Bryan Hall flushed, and there was the edge of temper in his tone. "I own no cattle, but I am the cashier of the bank, and I could remind you that the bank has cattle loans out to almost every man here. Of course I'm interested. In a way I have a deeper interest than anyone else."

Owen looked at him. Bryan was being pompous as usual. Bryan did not own the bank. As cashier he ran it, but it was a community affair. Old Joe John had helped start it, and Joe John had sold stock to the whole valley. It was supposedly run by a board of directors. Owen himself sat on this board, in Joe John's place, but he knew that in reality Bryan ran the institution as thoroughly as if he owned all of the stock.

He said in an even tone, "I'm sorry, Bryan. I didn't mean to be short with you, but I didn't expect to find any opposition. Surely none of us want to see four hundred people starve?"

"Indians?" The question came from a huge bearded man at the rear of the room. "I hate Indians."

Owen held his temper, and he spoke directly to the bearded man. "I heard you, Pete Daily, and I well remember the time you first rode up to the Box M. You didn't have two copper coins to knock together, and your feet were coming through your boot soles."

Dailey flushed, started to answer, then thought better of it and remained silent. Owen took a deep breath. "I hate to remind all of you of this, but there is not one person in the valley who does not owe something to Joe John. When Joe John came into this country, long before the war, it was all Indian land. There wasn't another settler within two hundred miles.

"He brought his cattle in, cattle he had traded from the Mexicans for furs. He brought in twenty head, and there is hardly a cow here today that isn't descended from those twenty head."

No one spoke. They stirred restlessly and after a moment he went on. "Joe John was here first, and he had the Indians to help him. He could have claimed the whole valley and gotten away with it. A lot of men claimed as much or more territory and held it, and they didn't have the natural barrier that this valley has."

He sensed the growing hostility of those facing him but he went on. "Joe John was no land hog. He welcomed each new settler. He helped you. Some of you rode for him and took your pay in stock, which he let run with his. He helped build your houses, helped found this town, and helped start the bank. He never asked one penny in return, although every new outfit cut his range that much more. The Box M used to run ten thousand head of stock. Now we hardly run two thousand, counting the she stuff and the calves. Think about it a minute, all of you."

They thought about it.

"So I'm collecting Joe John's debt. I want eight hundred steers. I want the strongest animals you have, the fattest. They won't be very fat by the time I get them up through the pass, that I warrant you. And I want volunteers. I can use a dozen men, more if they'll come. How about it?"

He stood waiting. He prayed that someone would come forward, anyone. If one man answered his call, others might be shamed into following.

The only man who moved was Bryan Hall. Grace Perkins was arguing with Hall, and Owen saw the flush of anger on the banker's face. Then Hall turned away from the girl and pushed through the crowd, stopping to speak to one man and then another.

Owen's eyes met those of Grace and he saw that there was no longer a glint of mirth in their grey depths. They looked sad, almost ashamed, and he realized that in this room he had at least one friend, one person who understood what he was trying to do.

His eyes hunted for Martha then, and he found her, near the corner, talking to Honos Walters and Stephen McBride and for a moment he had a lift, believing that she was supporting him, then he saw Bryan Hall join them and saw Martha nod her head at something which Bryan said, and smile at the banker, and knew that even Martha was set against him in this.

He had a deep, empty feeling of utter loss, and then he recalled again how Joe John had looked, and he raised his voice to still the murmur spreading across the hall.

"I'm not through," he said. "The agent has the gold to pay for the cows, and he will pay the price we asked in the fall. Not one of you will lose by it, that I promise."

Bryan turned. Bryan came back through the men and stopped, facing Tolliver, and the people gathered slowly behind him as if sensing a leader, as if sensing that someone would take up the argument for them.

"You promise they won't lose?" His tone was not quite jeering.

Owen thought with sudden surprise, Why, he's looking for a fight. He's angry. He's thoroughly angry, but he said soberly,

"I promise."

"Meaning that you will personally pay for all stock lost in the drive?"

He answered without thinking. "Why not?"

"What with?" said Bryan Hall, and there was a note of quick triumph in his voice. "How much money do you have, Owen, money of your own I mean, not from Joe John's estate, not money that belongs to your future wife?"

He said shortly, "Enough." He knew that the color had risen under the windburn which masked his cheeks.

"I question that," said Bryan Hall. "You forget, Owen, that I am the cashier at the bank, and I know to the penny the worth of every man in this room. You could not pay for fifty head and you well know it. Don't try to run a bluff in this, friend, not as you try to bluff at the card table."

Owen took half a step forward. His fists were knotted at his sides and a sudden red haze seemed to be floating in the air between him and Bryan Hall.

He heard Grace Perkins' voice from somewhere a long way distant saying, "No, Bryan, no, no!" and knew that Hall was charging toward him, and set himself for the attack.

They came together with a force which seemed to shake the building, two strong men, both near the same weight, both young and filled with rage.

Owen caught Hall's first blow high on his cheek and felt the skin split under the impact, and ducked his head, driving in with both fists, working them like pistons.

It could not last long. No one could hold the pace. He beat his fists upon Hall's ribs and took much punishment to the head in return, feeling his nose pulp under Hall's knuckles, blinded by a trickle of blood which ran down from a cut over his eye.

It was Hall who clinched. He had marked Tolliver far more than he had taken marks, but the steady pounding to the body sapped his strength, and he suddenly wrapped both long arms about Tolliver and they went to the floor together, rolling over and over before a dozen pairs of hands seized them and, pulling them apart, dragged them to their feet.

Owen looked around at the ring of faces and found no friendship there, and wiped his mouth with the back of his hand, drawing a blood streak across his cheek.

"I'll be around in the morning," he said when he had his breath. "I'll have a list of the stock I want. If you won't give it, I'll take it."

They glared back at him, but it was Bryan Hall who answered. "Don't try it." The words were nearly a gasp because of the shortness of his wind. "Don't try it, friend Owen. You aren't Joe John. You can't run this valley as if you were God. Take one cow without the owner's permission and we'll hang you as a rustler. That is a promise."

Owen looked at him levelly, seeing the raw desire in the depths of the man's dark eyes. And suddenly he had the feeling that he had never before actually known Bryan Hall.

He checked the words which rose to his lips, and

turning, walked over to where Martha stood a little removed from the rest of the crowd. Her eyes condemned him as he came up, and the anger which was at the instant latent within him warmed and threatened to flare anew, but he said in a tight voice,

"Ready?"

She said tonelessly, "I'm not going yet." Her manner told plainly that she was not going with him. He did not answer. He swung toward the entrance hall without a word, got his coat and hat from the row of pegs on the wall and went down the wide stairs toward the street. He heard someone behind him but did not look back. He pushed open the door, having to struggle against the wind, and then heard someone call his name from above.

He halted, turning slowly to see Karl Zeeman coming down the steps, and waited for the marshal to join him.

"Talk to you a minute?" The marshal's thin face was expressionless.

Tolliver shrugged and together they moved into the coldness of the night and wordlessly covered the distance to the Star. The saloon was empty save for the bartender, who read a week old paper, leaning his elbows on the scarred counter. He served them, staring without comment at Tolliver's battered face.

They ignored him and carried the drinks to a rear table. There Zeeman said, "I know what you're trying to do, boy, but it won't work."

There was a hot intemperate look in the eyes which

Tolliver raised to him. "Why not? Are we going to sit quiet and let those people starve?"

"You can't force these men to let you have their cattle, and if you try to take them I'll be on the other side of the fence." It was a warning. "Joe John ran this valley with a pretty high hand, Owen, but he never in his life did anything outside the law."

Tolliver's voice was harsh. "If he'd been there tonight they wouldn't have refused him."

"No."

"And they wouldn't have refused me if I had talked to them independently, one at a time."

"No."

Tolliver swallowed his drink at a gulp. "I can't understand Bryan Hall. What's eating him? I know he never liked me, but why should he take this time to make an issue? They aren't his cattle. What made him fight?"

The older man looked at him. "Don't you honestly know?"

Owen Tolliver hesitated, not meeting his eyes. Zeeman said slowly, "This isn't my business, I guess, but I'm a peace officer and there isn't going to be much peace around here until this is straightened out and you know what you're up against. I'll tell you what's troubling Bryan. It's Martha."

Tolliver shrugged, saying dully, "He's engaged to Grace Perkins."

"After it was announced that Martha would marry you."

They sat in silence for a long moment. "But why tonight?"

"Tonight," said Zeeman, "while you were talking to Walters before the dance, Martha talked to Bryan."

Tolliver did not move.

"She told him about the Indians. She told him that you had to be stopped before you stampeded the valley into driving those cattle. If I know Bryan, he saw the chance he's been looking for, the chance to drive a wedge between you and Martha. He was her champion tonight, Owen, and he had to prove to her that he is the better man. That's why he took the lead against you. That's why he heckled you into that senseless fight. He wanted to show you up as a fool."

"I see."

"Do you?" said Zeeman. "You might get the cattle you need if you rode around tomorrow, ranch to ranch, talking to each man on his own place. Few could stand alone against you, or against the memory of Joe John."

"You think so?"

"But be sure to give a promise to pay as soon as you have collected from the Indian agent. Be sure to get a bill of sale for every head. If I hear of you taking one cow otherwise, I'll come after you. We aren't going to have a war here in the valley."

Tolliver was looking through him. It was as if he had not heard the last lines. "You're sure about Martha? You're certain she put Bryan against me?"

There was pity in Zeeman's hard face. "I heard her," he said. "Better think it over, Owen, better decide.

Which do you want most, Martha, or to help those Indians?"

CHAPTER 4

I T WAS SNOWING AGAIN when Owen pulled into the ranch yard of the Box M, just after daylight. Smoke made its small plume from the tin chimney of the cookshack and there was a stir in the bunkhouse. He turned the horse into the shed, pulled off the saddle and hanging it over the side of the stall, moved stiffly toward the bunkhouse.

Hot air rushed out to meet him as he opened the door, and Shorty, clad only in his red underwear, turned to see who it was and let out a whistle at sight of him.

"Hey, we didn't expect you until evening. What happened to your face?"

He came in. Mac and Porine stepped around the big center stove to stare at him. Porine was a sad faced Irishman with a wicked mouth and a battered nose. Mac was short and square. Shorty was over six feet.

Porine was examining the knuckle marks with professional interest. "Boy, I quit going to the dances a year ago because they were so peaceful. Guess I made a mistake. Who marked you?"

Owen was stripping off his damp coat, hanging it before the stove, and he said shortly, "Bryan Hall."

Porine had all of the outdoor man's contempt for one who spent most of his life in a desk chair. "Well, knock me down, brother. Who would have thought it?

What's he look like?"

"Not as bad as I do." His tone was still short.

"You mean he's alive?"

"They pulled us apart."

Porine shook his head. "I knew I never did like that town. Let's ride back and finish the job."

Tolliver looked at him and slowly returned Porine's grin. He had no illusions about the man. Porine had been on the Box M less than two years. He was a drinker and a gambler and a drifter. He had never said where he came from, or where he was going.

From his battered features, from the way he wore his gun, and the alert way he studied each room before entering, Tolliver guessed that the Irishman had known trouble aplenty down the trail.

But he had caused no difficulty at the ranch. He did his work in an adequate manner, and nothing more. Shorty and Mac were a different breed. Shorty and Mac had been on the Box M for most of their lives.

They belonged to the group of men who lived their lives out in bunkhouses all over the West, who served the brand they rode for with an unquestioning and unimaginative devotion, who had no personal ambitions of their own and no plans for the future past the next payday.

He stood there, studying them all, and said finally to Porine, "So, you're spoiling for a fight?"

The man's grin widened. One of his front teeth had been snapped off halfway in some forgotten battle and a gold cap had been added.

"Why not?" said Porine. "Anything to break the pattern of riding in the snow and throwing down hay for the cow brutes." He sat on a bunk edge to pull on his pants and then work his way into his boots.

"I've got a fight for you," Tolliver said, and watched interest grow in Porine's dark eyes as he lifted his head.

He told them then about the Indians, about Joe John's promise to the tribe, about the dance hall and his fight with Bryan Hall. He left out his talk with Zeeman, and Martha's part.

They listened with attention, Shorty and Mac because a promise made by Joe John was very binding upon them, Porine because his active mind had already moved beyond Tolliver's words, and he saw a chance for trouble and for fighting and for fun.

They move over to the cookshack, and breakfasted on beef and potatoes and beans. The food had been almost the same ever since Martha had moved to town. The cook was old, and without initiative or interest.

But Tolliver hardly noticed. He was already deep in plans. He told the cook, "Get the sled wagon loaded up, and rig an extra hitch. We'll put four horses to it, the biggest we've got. Plenty of blankets and a canvas fly for shelter. It will be cold, up through the pass."

The cook grunted and showed his dissatisfaction. "You're not going," Tolliver said, understanding his reluctance to expose his rheumatic old bones to the cold. "You're needed here. We'll fill the racks and get the hay down, but you'll have to see that the snow is knocked away so the stock can get to it while we're gone."

Shorty said, "How much of our own beef goes?"

Tolliver consulted the list he'd made. "There are twenty brands in the valley, counting the ten cow out-fits, and we're the biggest. The way I have it figured from last fall's roundup, we'll take a hundred head from the Box M. It will scale down from there. Lucky I kept the tally sheets. No one can argue that he's being asked to throw in more than his share."

Mac had a slow mind and he said, "They stood against you last night, Owen. Why won't they stand against you today?"

Tolliver shrugged. "I'll try to talk them into it, Mac. I'll try to show them where their duty lies. A group of men can refuse, knowing that the brunt of the refusal falls on no one individual. One man hates to stand alone in anything. I think they will go along, especially if I've already gathered a few cows before I ride into their yard."

Porine said curiously, "And how will you persuade the first?"

Tolliver flashed the Irishman a look. Porine, he realized, was smart, much smarter than he had thought him in the past. He went right to the heart of things with every word.

"I'll hit the little outfits first," he said. "The brush-jumpers on the valley fringe, the men who are tolerated but not quite accepted. They aren't certain of their position. They know they've been suspected of wet branding now and then. They won't hesitate too long, and if I can ride into the yard of one of the bigger owners driving fifty to a hundred head in front of me, he'll be easier to talk to."

Porine's grin was wicked. "I always said you'd make a good poker hand if you gave your full attention to the game."

Owen Tolliver did not return the grin. This morning it seemed that the humor had been squeezed out of him. He could think of only one thing. Martha had failed him when he had needed her most. Martha had not come up to what he thought Joe John's daughter should.

They rode, Mac and Porine and Tolliver. They left Shorty to help the cook, to get the sled into shape, to get the hay down and cut out the hundred head the Box M was to furnish.

The ranch lay in a small canyon's mouth directly under the south rim, and the valley stretched before it, with Benton near the center and the pass leading to the reservation in the north end.

They hit Cantwines' first, and Owen Tolliver felt a little more secure that Porine rode at his back as they entered Cantwine's yard.

Cantwine was unpredictable, a man in his early forties, lean and hard and sardonic, a man who laughed at threats and had bragged openly that he had never yet eaten a single beef that carried his own brand.

In another community he might have been driven out long before, but Joe John, with the forbearance which characterized him, had let Cantwine alone. As long as the man contented himself with butchering an occasional Box M steer he winked at his presence and even hired him and his half-brother as extra hands during roundup.

It was snowing heavily as they swung into the yard, icy pellets which rattled like shot off the backs of their coats. Tolliver had his handkerchief up around his mouth, and another bound over his hat so that the wide felt brim was pulled down across his ears in an effort to keep out the biting cold.

The snow curtain was so thick that they couldn't see Cantwine's cabin or barns from the gate, and were almost in the yard before the two mangy hounds stirred themselves from their warm coop to give the alarm.

They rode directly for the house, and the door came open as they pulled up and Cantwine stood in the entrance. He was tall and thin, his face hawk-like because of his enormous nose, and he grinned when he saw the three riders who resembled nothing so much as mounted snow men.

"Fine, beautiful weather for a social call."

Tolliver swung down stiff-legged. The cold had eaten into the very center of his bones and he felt that every movement might break some vital part. He motioned to Mac to lead the horses over to the shelter of the shed, and tramped into the overheated room with Porine behind him.

The place was a mess of gear, of stacked canned goods and strewn clothing, and the smell which came out of it might have done credit to a bears' den. He slammed the door and pulled the handkerchief down from his mouth, and wiped away the ring of frost which his breath had made across his unshaven cheeks.

"This isn't a social call, Ray."

"I judged not," Cantwine said, and moved over to push the blackened coffee pot to the fore part of the stove. "Even Owen Tolliver has more sense than to ride for fun in this weather."

Tolliver untied the handkerchief which bound his hat, and stuffed it into his pocket, and loosened his coat, peeling it off against the time when he would have to go out again into the cold.

"You know why I'm here."

Cantwine's eyes were a little too close together, and the bridge of his nose was so high that it was difficult for him to look at a man unless he was facing him directly. The half-brother stirred in a far corner, offering no greeting, and a Mexican Tolliver had never seen before sat huddled beside the stove, not moving, not looking up.

"The Indians?" Cantwine had been at the dance.

"The Indians."

"The ranchers turned you down." There was a light of mockery in the tall man's eyes. "They forgot Joe John and his ways pretty quick, didn't they? A man dies, and in three months it is as if he had never lived."

"I'm not taking the turn-down," Tolliver said. The warmth from the stove had drawn some of the stiffness from his fingers. "I'm driving a herd over the pass, eight hundred head."

Cantwine considered. "If you get through."

"I'll get through." Tolliver said this with more confidence than he really felt. He wondered just how long the snow could continue. There had to be an end sometime.

"And what do you want from me?"

"Twenty head." He drew the fall roundup tally sheets from his pocket. "It's all here, every cow and steer we found in the valley. I've apportioned it."

"And you come to me first." The edge of mockery in Cantwine's tone was clearly audible. "Why?"

"Because you're one of the closest to the Box M."

"No," said Cantwine. "You come because you know I don't dare refuse you."

Tolliver did not grin. "And I'll never be certain that the steers I take didn't once run beside Box M cows."

"That you've never proved." Cantwine was still smiling.

"No. Joe John never would let me. You've gotten by for a long time, Ray. If it hadn't been for Joe John the other ranchers would have cleared you and the hill outfits off long ago. Now Joe John is dead."

The smile had gone from Cantwine's face, leaving it a little bleak, a little old looking. "And you are telling me that if I expect you to stand in Joe John's shoes and protect me from the others, I'd better throw in twenty cows."

"I'm telling you nothing, and promising you nothing. I'm merely saying that I've apportioned the number of cows I need, and I need twenty from you."

Cantwine looked at him for a long moment. "You win," he said. "Charley," he turned to his watching half-brother, "take the Mex and cut out twenty head. Make them the best we have."

His brother rose and took a coat from the peg and struggled into it.

Tolliver had not expected such an easy surrender. He said, "I want a bill of sale for those cows."

Cantwine was surprised. "Getting very legal all of a sudden."

"I'll give you a promise in writing that you will be paid as soon as I get the gold from the Indian agent."

"I'll take your word, Owen."

"No," said Tolliver. "This has to be on paper, in black and white."

Cantwine's smile was back in place. He said softly, "If I didn't know better I'd think you were accusing me of planning a trick."

Owen Tolliver shrugged, and after a moment Cantwine said, "Have it your way." He found a scrap of paper and pen and ink, and they sat at the littered table, making up the list. Then Cantwine got his coat and they went out into the weather. The snow still fell, but it had thinned enough so that they could see the buildings and the hay ricks.

It stopped two hours later, just as they came out of Turner's place under the southeast bench. Before them they drove nearly a hundred head, and Tolliver was glad that Cantwine and his brother had accompanied them.

He could not understand Cantwine's presence. The man had said simply, "We'll ride along."

Tolliver had looked at him, a question in his eyes, and Cantwine had grinned. "I want to see how some of my neighbors take it when you come after their cattle. Their faces should be worth watching."

Owen Tolliver had considered him. He had never known Ray Cantwine well and did not like what he had known. He said, "You must enjoy watching others suffer to be willing to ride against this snow just for that pleasure."

"Why not?" said Cantwine. "All my life I've hated the full human race. No man ever did me a service that I know of, unless it was Joe John who merely tolerated me."

There was a bitter note under the laugh which made Tolliver look at him questioningly. Then he shrugged and saying, "Your business," headed the cattle out of Cantwine's yard.

At Grover's they picked up forty head. Grover was a silent man and he made little objection now, saying only, "You're forcing me to do this, Owen."

"I'm asking you," Owen said.

"You're forcing me," Grover insisted. "Next summer when Salt Creek goes dry I'll be throwing my bunch onto your grass as I've always done. If I don't help you now, my cattle will starve in the hot weather."

Tolliver did not answer. He felt the reproachful eyes of Grover's wife as her husband signed the bill of sale, and heard her mutter in her dry, drab tone,

"Indians, all for Indians, and the Indians killed my father long ago."

He did not look at her. There was a weariness in her voice and a small note of heartbreak there. These cattle which he was taking represented five years of work for them, hard work, bitter work. The margin on which they lived was slim indeed, but in the whole valley no one was rich, no one had cows to throw away.

"I'll get them through," he promised. "You'll be paid in full."

He knew by their expressions that they did not believe him. He knew that they thought they were looking at the worth of their cattle for the last time as he drove them out and added them to Cantwine's animals, which Porine was holding in the snowy roadway.

He almost turned back. Then he remembered the Indians beyond the pass. He remembered Joe John, and he pushed on.

CHAPTER 5

THE RECEPTION was far different at the Daily place. For one thing, the Daily ranch was the biggest they had yet hit, and Pete Daily in his own way had always considered himself something of a leader in the valley and a rival for Joe John's position.

Pete had been the first Box M foreman, and he had taken his wages in cows, and after six years he had married and set himself up where Snake Creek broke through the barrier and fought its twisting way down the upedged rock of the lower bench to reach the level floor.

In summer it was a pretty spot, with the trees on the bench behind it and the weathered buildings looking almost silver against the green carpeting of the stream's course above.

The bunch of cattle they were driving had grown close to the two hundred mark. The snow had stopped entirely, the grey clouds had split, and the sun came through to turn the world into a sparkling thing which hurt men's eyes, and could if long endured bring on a form of blindness.

Owen Tolliver had left the Cantwines to bring up the cows, and with a rising impatience pushed on to Daily's, Porine and Mac behind him.

This, he realized, was the big test. If Daily fell in line, Honos Walters would follow and the fight would be won, for Pete and Honos were the two biggest owners in the valley after the Box M itself.

He turned into the snow covered lane and knew suddenly that the news of his arrival had preceded him, for Daily and his two sons and his son-in-law were standing in the yard, and they all held rifles.

Daily was known to be a close man, and his winter crew had each year been composed of his relatives and of no outside rider, and Tolliver frowned, not needing Porine's low voice comment as the Irishman said, "Trouble."

He pulled around the poles of the corral fence, riding

to where Daily stood watching him, and made no effort to dismount, only easing his weight in the saddle and trying to break some of the stiffness which the cold had carried to his bone centers.

"Afternoon, Pete."

There was no smile of greeting on Pete Daily's face. With his black whiskers, touched with breath-frost, he looked something like an aging, discontented porcupine as he shifted the rifle into the crook of his left arm.

Tolliver nodded at the gun. "Going hunting?"

Daily said, "Just want to make certain that none of our cows stray."

"I'm sure you do." Tolliver's voice was soft. "Want to talk out here or can we have a bit of warmth from the stove?"

Daily's anger showed in his thin voice. "Owen," he said, "you are wrong in this and we both know it, and there's no use talking, here or by the stove. You aren't taking one head from my place."

Owen Tolliver schooled his temper. He said quietly, "I'm not taking cows from anyone, Pete. I'm not a rustler."

"You said last night . . ."

"Several things were said last night that would have been better left unsaid. We've all lived in this valley for some time, and we are all apt to be here for quite a spell more. We don't want a feud developing that might carry on senselessly for years."

"The trouble isn't of my making." Daily's tone was harsh.

"Nor of mine," said Tolliver. "But we all have to live with our consciences, Pete. How are you going to feel next spring, knowing that four hundred people died of hunger because you wouldn't risk eighty of your cows?"

"Indians."

"Meaning that if those people on the reservation had white skins you wouldn't hesitate?"

Pete Daily blew out his breath explosively. "Of course not. What kind of a man do you think I am?"

"I'm not judging you," Owen Tolliver said. "I'm leaving you to judge yourself. This is a community project, Pete, and if we all throw in together on it, all help, the valley will be the stronger for it, even if we lost every single head in the drive. Can't you see that? Can't you realize that in this country we all need each other, just as the Indians need help at the moment? How would you feel if the boot were on the other foot, if your wife and kids and grandkids were starving and if the Indians up there had cows and wouldn't sell you any?"

As he talked he let his gaze shift to Pete's sons, and saw the uncertainty in their faces, and knew that none of them were as determined as they had been, and he went on.

"I'm asking you to throw eighty head into the herd. Eighty head won't break you, even if you lost them, and there is no need that they be lost. Let your two boys and your son-in-law ride with me. We'll get through, and you'll get a fair price for your stock, and you'll have the knowledge that you did the right thing, even if it is merely a bunch of Indians you helped."

Daily spat. "Damn you, Owen, you have a way with words. You put a man in the wrong even when he knows he is right."

Tolliver did not relent. "I've already gathered two hundred head. They come from the little outfits along the bench, men you despise because they have less than you have, men you distrust because you believe they may sometimes have been careless with your stock. These men are going to be proud of what they have done, even if they were a little reluctant at first to go along. They're going to look down on you. They are going to remember, each time you try to lead anything, that you are the man who refused to send any cattle through the pass."

"Damn you."

Tolliver shrugged. He had never studied salesmanship, but he sensed that he had talked enough, that any word he added would now hurt his cause.

"It's up to you," he said. "We've got to move." He turned his horse then as if certain that Daily's refusal would stand, as if he meant to ride out of the yard.

Daily let him get a dozen paces, then with a muttered oath he started forward. "Owen, wait."

Tolliver checked his horse. As he turned back he caught a fleeting grin on Porine's face and saw the Irishman wink.

"Damnit," said Daily as Tolliver came up. "You put a man in the wrong all the time."

Owen said nothing and the bearded man grunted. "Take them," he said. "Take them, and the boys can ride with you to see that they don't get buried in the snow." He turned toward his sons. "Cut out eighty head, and get your gear, and I'll have the skin off all of you if we lose a single steer."

He motioned for Owen to follow him and swung about, striding toward the house.

Owen got down, handing his reins to Porine. The Irishman said in an undertone, "You've won, but you've made yourself an enemy for life. No man likes being in the wrong, and no man likes the knowledge that another put him there."

"I didn't."

"No, he did it to himself. And on top of that you made him back down. He'll never forgive you, not in this world or in the next."

Inside, the Daily house was clean and warm and bright with half a dozen grandchildren under foot, staring up at Tolliver out of black, watchful eyes.

Pete got down the paper and pen as Tolliver asked, and laboriously wrote out the bill of sale. His wife watched him from the kitchen door, and her two daughters-in-law kept carefully out of sight.

It was the manner in which Mrs. Daily looked at him that hurt Tolliver. As a boy she had mothered him when the roundup crew was working the Daily land; and he had a genuine affection and respect for her.

He wrote out his promise that as soon as the gold was collected from the Indian agent he would pay for the eighty head, and saying goodbye, moved toward the door.

No one answered him. No one spoke as he stepped out onto the snowy porch and went to the big holding corral where the riders were bringing up the stock from the winter pasture. He watched the animals struggle as they breasted the snow which in places was deeper than the length of their stout legs, and knew a sharp doubt that they would ever reach the pass, let alone climb through it to the reservation beyond.

He had a swift impatient desire to be a thousand miles from there, to be in a land where you never heard of cows, or Indians, or snow. He reached his own horse and stepped up into the saddle. The wind bit at his ears as he pulled out the handkerchief and tied it in place and thus deadened the bawling of the worried animals.

He turned, noting unconsciously that another cloud bank was building up toward the east, and that it seemed colder than it had an hour before.

There was the smell of more snow in the air. He wondered how much longer it could last. Never in his twenty-five years had he seen as much snow in the valley as was there at the moment.

Far off down the twisting road was the black blot of the cattle which Cantwine was driving slowly forward. With Daily's steers he would have nearly three hundred head, and he had the thought that he would have to find a place for them that night, and decided on Zeigler's ranch.

He wished that the gather could have been made in a

single day, for he dreaded the evening, with the possibility that the owners might get together and some of them change their minds.

The Dailys had the stock bunched now, and Porine and Mac were moving them out along the lane toward the road. He went forward to help, knowing that Daily's sons would have to stop to collect their gear and could join them later.

They'd make Zeigler's, he thought, and get fifty head there, and feed the stock at his ricks. They'd bed down in the barn and make an early start in the morning. But he would not stay with them. He'd cut back to the Box M and help Shorty and the cook bring up the hundred head from the home ranch. Porine could handle things at Zeigler's over night. Or could he?

There might be an argument, and the last thing they needed at the moment was a fight. Better to send Porine back while he himself stayed with the cattle. There would be far less chance for trouble in that way.

He rode on, planning, and he did not hear what Porine said, nor did he notice the group of horsemen coming from the north. He did not see them until they had travelled a good three miles, nor would it have mattered if he had, for there was no turning back and no escape.

CHAPTER 6

GRACE PERKINS left the restaurant and paused at Bailey's store and then moved on to Libell's bakery and afterward, her arms laden with packages, she stopped in at the bank.

She kicked the snow from her overshoes and put down her bundles on the bench beside the door. The long narrow room with its single teller's cage was warm from the fat stove in the corner, and the wide front windows were so laced with frost patterns that it was impossible to see through them.

Gilbert North, the teller, looked through his wicket and smiled at her, and nodded to the empty desk in the rear corner, saying, "He went down the street five minutes ago. He said he'd be back in a bit."

She nodded and moved to the wooden railing which separated Bryan Hall's domain from the rest of the bank, and pushing open the low gate, sat down in the visitor's chair.

Her eyes went to the ordered top of the polished desk, with its two penholders carefully laid beside the heavy inkwell. The desk, she thought, represented Bryan Hall's conception of life itself, a meticulous thing, molded by habit and by tradition, a pattern that was never broken except in the case of absolute emergency.

Hall came in then, bringing a swirl of windswept snow with him, his face beneath the even line of his black hat reddened by the cold so that his eyes seemed much bluer than they really were. For a moment he did not see her as he shucked out of his coat and stood with it over his arm, warming his hands before the stove.

Then he turned, and the smile came, just as she had known it would, and she found herself examining that smile, wondering how much of it was spontaneous and how much a polite performance of a duty.

This was not her first doubt of him. She had experienced others in the past, but she had put them aside, supposing that every woman now and then must entertain some reservations about the man she is to marry.

She was too honest a person to dissemble, and she felt a little guilty as she rose to greet him, saying in a quick, breathless voice,

"I know how much you dislike being disturbed during business hours, but I felt that I had to talk to you."

He came through the gate and hung his coat and hat upon the tree, and smiled again as he sat down at the desk.

"I'm sorry you had to wait."

"It was only a minute."

"I had to see Parkingstead about his loan." He was always careful to account for his time. She found the habit slightly embarrassing, a school boy's attitude of explaining himself to a teacher.

"I wanted to talk to you about last night."

She saw his face tighten and go blank, his eyes turn a little hard, and she hurried on. "I didn't sleep very much, Bryan, thinking about those Indians. The boy who brought the word stayed in the storeroom last night. I gave him breakfast before he left. It was painful to hear his confidence. He was so certain that Tolliver would save his people."

Bryan Hall said, "Owen Tolliver had no right to promise him anything. Owen takes too much upon himself. He always has."

"Someone had to take the lead." She was trying to be reasonable. "Would you have felt differently about this, Bryan, if the Indian had come to you?"

He said pompously, "That has nothing at all to do with it, believe me. If I thought there was even a moderate chance of getting those cattle through, I would have backed Tolliver last night."

"Would you, Bryan?"

He flushed. "What do you mean?"

She said, "I'm not trying to quarrel with you. I detest people who quarrel, but I could not help overhearing Martha Martel when she talked to you last night. I could not help knowing that she was using you because she was opposed to sending the cattle, and yet lacked the courage to tell Owen Tolliver so in plain words."

His face was redder still. "You shouldn't blame Martha. Owen Tolliver can be very stubborn at times."

"I'm not blaming Martha." She was fighting to keep her control. "I'm not even judging her, since it is not my place to judge. But I do object to her using you as a cat'spaw. I do object to your doing something in which you can't possibly believe, because she asks you to."

He was thoroughly angry now. "No one is using me as a cat'spaw as you put it. I did what I did because I felt that the whole economy of the valley was being threatened. These people work very hard for what they get, and none of them are rich. Supposing I were to ask you to give say a third of what you have in the restaurant. Would you do it?"

"If others were starving, yes."

He bit his lip. He was a man who, despite his explosive action at the dance, seldom permitted himself an open quarrel.

"No one wants anyone to starve," he said, "but neither do I think it fair to penalize all of the people in this valley because a stupid Indian agent made a mistake." He broke off then, for the outer door had banged open and half a dozen excited men tramped in.

He turned in annoyance, frowning. Grover was in the lead and Grover was talking angrily. "I tell you he forced me to. He might as well have put a gun at my head. He took the cows, didn't he? Isn't that what counts? He took the cows."

Bryan Hall was on his feet. He pushed open the gate and stepped through, coming face to face with the men. "What's this about?"

Grover told him. The injustice had been riding him ever since Tolliver had left his place. "He took my cows," he finished. "He'd been to the Cantwines and to all the other small outfits under the south rim, and he was heading for Daily's the last I saw of him, driving two hundred head."

Bryan Hall swore under his breath.

Grover said in a plaintive voice, "He's like a wolf, or an Indian. He just looks at you, and you know you can't stop him. Me, I need Box M grass when Salt Creek runs dry. I can't stand against him."

Bryan Hall said, "I'll promise you that you won't be cut out of grass next dry season just because you didn't go along with Owen Tolliver. We've got to get word to the ranchers north on this. The valley will have to stand together."

"Ike Homes and Bill Stuart have already ridden up that way. They sent me in to tell you."

"All right."

"They'll bring the ranchers in. Will you ride with us, Mr. Hall? We need someone to talk for us."

Grover was ten years older than Bryan Hall, and had known him all his life, and had never in the full time addressed him as Mister.

It was an unconscious acknowledgment of Hall's leadership that the word had slipped out, and slipped out unnoticed. But Bryan Hall noticed, and it sent a warm feeling of achievement running through him.

He had a machine-like mind, and from the very beginning he had planned how he would make his place in the valley. And he had chosen well. No one else had wanted the position in the bank. They were outdoor men, with no understanding of the real functions of a bank, no understanding of the power which money as a useful tool would give.

But Bryan Hall had understood, and he had leaped at

58

the chance when it had come. The other alternative would have been to stay on the poor ranch which his father owned, up under the north rim, close to the entrance to the pass.

He had started in the bank as teller, under old Joe Russell who had once run the town's store, and whom Joe John had seated in the cashier's chair for want of a better man.

But he had not remained teller long, and from the very first the real authority was in his hands. He had used it sparingly, watchfully, careful not to make enemies, careful that the cattle owners who sat upon his board believed that the decisions which he steered them into were taken on their own initiative.

He had watched the deposits grow, and watched the loans develop, and watched the capital with a clear eye. Very little of it was his personal property, but he husbanded it as if every dollar was in his own account.

For he wanted power. He dreamed of the time when this whole valley would be his, when by foreclosure and careful buying the bank would own most of the range surrounding Benton.

He did not know when he had first had the idea. It came to him gradually, as he considered how foolish old Joe John was. Joe John had controlled the valley once, and he had given it away, because Joe John had liked people and because Joe John had held that everyone should have their chance.

It was a feeling which Bryan Hall had never shared. He had nothing but contempt for the weak. To him the world was a place to be seized by the strong, and held by the strong, and ruled by the strong. The bank was his strength and he meant to use it to the fullest, but he had other, secondary plans, and the foremost of these concerned Martha Martel.

He supposed that in his own way he had always loved the girl. Certainly he had found pleasure in her company, but it was a pleasure salted with the knowledge that her father owned the largest ranch in the valley, the biggest block of stock in the bank. When the time came, he planned to use these holdings as a springboard for further operations.

He had known from the first that Owen Tolliver stood in his way, both with Martha and with his plans for the valley. But in his single mistake he had discounted Tolliver, too certain of his standing with the girl.

When it was announced that she and Tolliver would marry he had, for the first time in his life, lost his head. He was convinced that the action was prompted not by Martha's feelings, but by Joe John's decree, and he set himself to make Martha jealous by paying marked attention to Grace Perkins.

He thought about Grace now as he walked back toward her. She was attractive, probably the most attractive girl in the valley, after Martha, but there was a spirit of independence in her which worried him.

Nor had Martha reacted as he had expected. If Martha felt any jealousy for his new interest, she concealed it well. She had in fact rather gone out of her way to make a friend of Grace, and he had been considering means of breaking his engagement without hurting himself in the eyes of the valley people when September had come, and Joe John was thrown from his horse, and Owen Tolliver was in Joe John's saddle.

Bryan Hall hated Tolliver. He knew now that the hatred ran back deep into their childhood. But it had been fanned into quick flame by recent happenings. Tolliver was to marry Martha. Tolliver from Joe John's position on the bank board had asked embarrassing questions about loans, questions which had never been asked before.

He had watched, waiting for Tolliver to make a mistake, waiting until he could stand against him with the valley in support behind him.

And he knew that his time had now come, that this absurd plan to drive cattle through the snow of the pass to the reservation played directly into his hands. Not one voice in the valley had been raised to commend Owen in this idea, not even Martha's.

And he would use this to talk to Martha, to point out subtly to her that he, not Owen, was better fitted to be her husband, better fitted to run the Box M, better fitted to run the bank.

His concentration on his own thoughts was so intense that for the instant he forgot Grace's presence and was startled as she said in a low voice,

"You aren't riding with them, Bryan, you aren't taking a hand in this?"

He looked at her, and his face was empty with stupid

surprise for an instant, then he said carefully, "I think that you and I need a slightly better understanding."

"I'm certain of it." Her tone was without inflection. "I heard you tell Grover a minute ago that you would wait for the ranchers from the northern rim and then ride out with them."

"Your hearing is remarkably acute." He allowed himself a tinge of sarcasm. "What else did you expect me to do after last night?"

She said, "I didn't expect you to act the way you did last night. I still do not understand. I am beginning to think that I don't know you, that I never actually knew you."

He was filled with a great impatience. He wished that she would go. He had a number of things which he wanted to do, and not too much time to do them. But he forced himself to answer her calmly, to try to reason with her. He was not ready for an open break with her, at least not yet, not until more of the cards were in his hands, the game more definitely coming his way.

He said quietly, "This valley is a community, and the heart of the community is the town, and the heart of the town is this bank. And I am, for all practical purposes in most men's eyes, the bank."

"But still . . ."

He said, "A moment more. I took the action I took last night because most of the people around us are nearly wordless, they need a voice."

"A voice which will let hungry people starve?" There was almost an edge of contempt in her tone. He heard it and flushed slightly.

"Grace," he said, "you're young, and you are emotional, and I like you for it. But the world cannot run on emotion. We must be practical. Someone has to think of the needs and wants of the people in this valley, to realize that they too can be in danger, that they have a certain right to self protection."

She said in a tired voice, "When you start burying your thoughts in words I begin to be afraid. Clever men do that, Bryan. Are you trying to be a clever man?"

He winced, drawing a shield over his eyes in an attempt to keep her from reading his thoughts. But he said, almost harshly, "Owen Tolliver is the clever man. I'm afraid that he's convinced you."

"I saw the Indian," she said. "Seeing him convinced me, as I think it did Owen."

She turned and pushed open the gate and walked out of the bank, and he made no effort to stop her, and knew by the set of her shoulders that whatever he had had there was gone, and that it would not return, and felt curiously relieved as if he were now free to take the next step in his move for power.

He sat down at the desk and pulled out the lower drawer, and lifted out the holstered gun. He weighed it in his hand, and then rising, strapped it about his hips.

He was not dressed for riding, so with a word to the teller he left the bank and walked along the partly cleared sidewalk to the hotel, where he maintained a permanent room.

He climbed the stairs, changed his clothes and came back down. He knew the impulse to see Martha, to let her know that he was still fighting for her, still trying to stop Owen Tolliver. But he decided against it and stepped out onto the wide, snow filled gallery.

Better not to rush things, better to let the trouble now between those two come to a head, better if the girl came to him. It would put him in a much more favorable position with her. She would be far more apt to listen to his counsel.

There was a crowd before the livery stable, and turning he saw a group of horsemen coming into town from the north. He went down the steps and back along the walk toward Parkingstead's. He did not feel the cold, nor the bite of the wind. His mind was fully occupied with the future.

The men before the livery parted to let him pass and Grover said excitedly, "Here come the others. Now we'll see."

They looked at Bryan Hall questioningly. He felt the weight of their uncertainty and knew that this was his moment.

In a little while he would ride out of town with ten to twelve men at his back, and they would pick up others on their way south. He did a quick sum in his head. They should have at least twenty by the time they faced Owen Tolliver, twenty men, representing nearly every outfit it the valley.

And from that moment all hope Tolliver might have entertained of stepping effortlessly into Joe John's shoes would be gone.

Bryan Hall smiled without mirth as he threw a saddle onto a horse and prepared to lead it out. Tolliver had had everything that a man might wish in life handed to him, and he had thrown it away by this one silly gesture. The man, Bryan Hall thought, must be stupider than he had ever imagined. He knew now that besides being jealous of Owen he had always been a little afraid of him. He thought with contempt that it was a mistake he would not make again.

He led out the horse as the men from the north rode up, and he was about to speak to them when Karl Zeeman came pushing through the crowd. He stared at the marshal with eyes suddenly gone bleak, saying quietly, "We can handle this without your help, Karl."

The marshal looked at him. The marshal looked at the faces of the others, feeling the grimness. The marshal sighed. "I don't think you can, Bryan. I don't think you could, or would, stop a lynching if Tolliver doesn't bow to you. And these men are in a lynching mood. I'll ride along."

CHAPTER 7

GRACE PERKINS watched through the front window of the restaurant as Bryan Hall passed it on his way to the hotel. She saw the men gathering about the entrance of the livery stable and in a kind of panic considered what she could do.

Panic was a new experience for her, since she had

always had a full measure of self-confidence. But now she felt completely helpless.

She saw fresh riders come in from the north to join the crowd at the stable and was of half a mind to follow them, to make an appeal, but she was too late, for Hall had joined them and they rode away to the south, Hall and the marshal riding in front.

It was then that she decided to see Martha Martel, and she hurried from the restaurant, not even waiting to put a shawl about her shoulders.

Martha was coming down the stairs into the lobby as Grace entered from the street, and they both stopped and for a moment stared at each other in strained silence before Grace said, "Did you see Bryan? Did you talk to him before he left?"

Martha shook her head and Grace told her quickly, "Then you don't know that they've ridden out to stop Owen?"

Martha nodded. "I guessed as much. What's he done now?"

"He's gathering a herd, as he said he would, last night."

"The fool."

"You mean Owen?"

"Of course I mean Owen. Once he gets an idea in his head he is as stubborn as an unbroken three-year-old horse. From what happened last night he should know that the valley is all against him."

Grace said, slowly, "You almost sound as if you are glad of it."

"I'm realistic," Martha told her. "I have to live with these people as neighbors."

Some of Grace's desperate fear showed in her voice. "That's not important now. Those men with Bryan are mad, and they're wearing guns. You don't want them to kill Owen, do you?"

Martha said with confidence, "I saw Karl Zeeman ride out with Bryan. There will be no shooting as long as Karl is along, but it's time that Owen learned a lesson. He is not my father, and he cannot run things with a high hand as my father did."

Grace was seeing this girl in a new light. "You are actually glad to see the valley stand against him, aren't you?"

Martha said, slowly, "I tried to tell him last night. He wouldn't listen. It is something that he must learn, to listen. Have you ever tried to make Bryan Hall listen to you?"

Grace flushed and the other girl laughed. "Men do not like to be told what to do, especially by a woman, but few marriages are successful unless the woman can assert herself."

Grace did not answer. At the moment she did not trust herself to speak. She turned and left the lobby without a word, and behind her heard Martha Martel laugh, saying in a mocking voice, "It's time to grow up, Grace. It's time to realize that men take managing."

Grace Perkins let the hotel door slam behind her and all the way back down the cold street she fought to control herself. But as she re-entered the restaurant it was obvious to her mother that something was the matter and she asked sharply,

"What's happened?"

Her daughter told her. "I'm not certain that I'm going to marry Bryan, that I ever want to marry anyone."

"You've had a fight with him," her mother said, "and the first fight is always painful."

"It's more than a fight. This is a matter of basic principle."

Her mother did not answer and Grace passed her, disappearing into the living quarters at the rear of the building. She came out, half an hour later, dressed for riding, wearing an old sheepskin lined coat of her father's.

Her mother looked at her in disapproval. "No woman with sense ever interferes in a man's game."

"I've got to try," Grace said. "I won't sit quietly by and wait for them to kill each other." She turned and left the restaurant, headed for the livery.

CHAPTER 8

THE CATTLE MOVED SLOWLY, not liking the footing, tending to bunch up and try to mill. Owen Tolliver rode ahead, with the Cantwine brothers beside him, their horses breaking the even whiteness of the drifted road, forming a tumbled path through which Mac and Porine and the Daily boys pushed the reluctant animals.

It was slow work, and they had covered less than half

a mile when they became conscious of the grouped horsemen coming toward them from the distant town.

Cantwine saw them first and his thin face, protected from the wind by the tied neck-cloth turned sardonic beneath the covering as he glanced at Tolliver.

Owen's head was down, his eyes upon the glistening whiteness as he tried to pick out the road line beneath the snow.

"We've got more help," said Cantwine and laughed his dry laugh. "Maybe the boys figured we couldn't drive these cows alone."

Tolliver's head came up and his eyes measured the approaching riders, and his shoulders which had been stooped against the wind stiffened. The riders were still too far away for him to be absolutely certain who they were, but one thing was obvious to Tolliver. Whoever they were they were not riding out to help.

He glanced sidewise at the Cantwines. Charley was as wordless as ever, apparently unconscious of any approaching danger. He was a strange character. In the dozen years Tolliver had known him he had heard the man utter less than twenty words. There were people in the valley who believed firmly that he could not speak. He was older than Ray, perhaps ten years older, and he never showed emotion of any kind. He rode now with his head still down against the wind, apparently not even conscious that anyone was coming.

Tolliver looked at Ray. He said, "If there's trouble, you and your brother drop back. This is not your fight. You can't afford to turn these men further against you."

For an instant there was a look of intolerance in Ray Cantwine's eyes, then it was gone and he said in cold humor, "I've been looking forward to a fight all day. I wouldn't miss this for the world."

The men behind the cattle had seen the oncoming riders also, and as Tolliver turned to look he saw one of the Daily boys pull his horse around and head toward the ranch they had recently left, and he thought, he's going for his father. He knows that there is a showdown coming and he wants Pete here to tell him what to do.

He said aloud to Charley Cantwine, "Drop back and send Porine up to me," and watched the man pull around obediently and heard Ray Cantwine murmur,

"That Porine looks like a good man for a fight."

Tolliver did not answer. He had not sent for Porine because he wanted the man to fight, but for exactly the opposite reason. He did not trust the explosive quality in Porine, the ever-present desire for battle. The last thing he wanted at the moment was to have a gun drawn, and he felt that he could control Porine better if the man were riding at his stirrup.

Porine came forward, his eyes on the road ahead, his mouth looking pleased as he said, "Looks like we've got a little company."

"No trouble," said Tolliver and looked at him, hard.

Porine's eyes were guileless. "Who thought of trouble, friend Owen? We are on a peaceful errand of mercy to the poor Indians." He winked at Cantwine and got a bland stare in return. Tolliver realized that neither of these men cared anything about the Indians, or the cattle. Both were pressed forward by an urge for violence, an urge they themselves could not explain.

He said, flatly, "There will be no trouble. The first man who touches a gun will answer to me. I won't have my former friends killed in the name of mercy."

Porine reminded him, "You may not have the full say on that, Owen. Bryan Hall is bound to try and take the play away from you." He glanced across his shoulder at the approaching riders who were now close enough to recognize.

Owen held up his hand so that the men behind would stop pressing the cattle and the small herd began to mill, turning their tails to the wind and drifting slightly. He shouted for the men to watch them and turned back to face the oncoming ranchers, not seeing Pete Daily spur out of his yard, followed by his son and race toward the herd, not conscious that Daily had almost reached him until Bryan Hall rode up with the ranchers at his back and called,

"Which side are you on, Pete?"

"My own," Daily answered promptly.

Owen Tolliver turned in the saddle and met Pete Daily's stare and saw that Daily was not troubling to hide his dislike, as he called, "Try your fancy words on them, Owen, as you did on me. I'm anxious to see how good you really are."

Tolliver did not answer. His eyes swept the mounted men, pausing for an instant as he saw Karl Zeeman at Hall's side, trying to figure what was best to say, and chose to address the marshal, ignoring Hall.

"I kept my promise, Karl." He unbuttoned his coat and showed the sheaf of papers in his inside pocket. "I have a bill of sale for every animal in this bunch."

Zeeman said in a neutral voice, "I don't doubt you have, Owen. This little junket was not my idea." He did not need to glance at Bryan Hall to show whose idea the trip had been.

Owen refastened a single button on his coat and drew the glove back onto his already stiffening hand and his voice was a sharp question. "Then maybe you all rode out to help us?"

Bryan Hall felt the play slipping away from him, and said furiously, "Owen, stop making double-talk. You know why we are here and what we intend to do."

"No," said Tolliver, "I can guess why you are here, and what you intend to do, but I'm not certain you'll do it."

Hall's hands tightened. "You think you were vastly clever, don't you, jumping on the small outfits, the men like Grover who dared not keep you from taking their stock because they draw a good part of their support from the Box M."

"I forced no one."

"That's a lie. You forced them as surely as if you had pulled a gun and put it against their heads, and I for one am not going to let you get away with it. All of them owe money to the bank, and if they lose these cattle they never can repay those loans."

Owen Tolliver's mind told him that he was fighting

a losing battle. He had sensed it when he had first seen Hall's party riding toward him, but his innate stubbornness would not allow him to quit.

His eyes ranged along the curving circle the riders made behind Bryan Hall and Karl Zeeman as if they expected him to try and drive the herd past them and meant to stop him, and he picked out Grover as the center for his attack, hating himself for the necessity, but knowing that he must direct his efforts toward the weakest link if he hoped to break the chain.

He did not raise his voice and did not need to, for he was the center of their full attention. He said, "I got some steers from you this morning, Grover, and you gave me a bill of sale. Did I force you to give me those cattle or that bill of sale?"

Grover wet his lips. Grover sent an appealing look toward Bryan Hall. Grover had expected safety in this crowd. Grover had not expected to be singled out by Tolliver for direct attack.

"Why," he said, "I . . . well . . . it seemed wisest to let you take the stock."

Bryan Hall said quickly, "Wasn't the reason you let him take those cows because you knew that you would need Box M grass next dry season? Didn't he blackmail you into giving them?"

"Well . . ."

"Did I mention the grass?" Tolliver's voice was tight. "If anyone mentioned it, it was you."

"Well, yes, but . . ."

Pete Daily had had enough. When his son had ridden

quickly back to the ranch to tell him that Hall's men were coming, he had been filled with sudden hope that the cows which he had already given up as lost were safe again. He pressed forward now, not willing to let this new found chance slip away.

"Stop it, Owen." He suddenly shoved his horse between Tolliver and Porine. "Stop it. You know that you raw-hided every man whose cows you took, including me. You forced us to sign."

Owen turned, knowing the game was lost. "I never thought that you'd back down on any promise you made, Pete. I thought your word, your signature was good."

The old man's wind-burned face took on a purple cast and his hand dropped quickly to his belted gun. But as his hand went down, Porine drew in one swift motion, and his long barrelled Colts was jammed in Daily's side and he was grinning as he said, "Don't do it, Pete. I'd love to blow you into kingdom come."

Bryan Hall lost his head. He drew before Zeeman at his side knew what he was about, and drove a shot at Porine which missed the rider's head by inches.

Zeeman made a grab for the banker's arm but missed as Hall's horse danced sidewise. Tolliver had no chance to draw in time, his hands were gloved, his coat buttoned, but he drove both spurs into his horse's flanks, jumping the animal directly at the banker.

Hall's gun went off, almost directly in his face, but Hall's spooked horse was dancing, and the shot went wild. He never fired another for Tolliver had the wrist above the gun solidly with both hands. He jerked and Hall came free of the saddle, the weight of his falling body pulling Tolliver from his own horse.

They went down together into the trampled snow. Around them the skittish horses plunged as their cursing riders tried to bring them under control, endangering the struggling men with their kicking hoofs.

To Owen Tolliver the sudden fight brought a welcome relief from the anger which had been building up within him since the night before. Bryan Hall had lost his gun in the downward plunge and it was now buried somewhere under the churned snow. He broke Tolliver's grip on his wrist somehow and rolled away, coming to his feet, crouching there for a moment, then charging with both arms swinging.

Tolliver came up to meet him, and threw an overhand left which exploded in Hall's face. Both men were hampered by the heavy coats they wore, but the anger of both was such that there was no stopping them.

The blow had halted Bryan Hall in his tracks, and brought blood to his bruised lips. He used a coat sleeve to wipe it away and then lowering his head charged like an angry bull.

Tolliver hit him twice on the side of the head as he came in, then Hall's arms wrapped about him and they went down together, rolling over and over in the snow until it was impossible for the watchers to tell one from the other.

Porine was not watching the struggling men. Porine still held his gun against Pete Daily's side. Porine had drawn it by impulse, his instinctive reaction to back up Tolliver. Now he was in a box, for although his gun was at Daily's side, holding the old man immobile, both of Daily's sons were behind him, and experience told him that he was in a bad spot.

He counted without Ray Cantwine. Cantwine had pulled to one side. Cantwine was not a man to enter a fight directly without counting the cost.

It was not that Ray Cantwine was a coward, but his life had been cast along devious paths and the fact that he was still alive spoke highly of his intuitive ability to choose the proper time and place for his every action.

He had pulled aside so that the Daily boys were not at his back, and he took his time drawing his gun, not wanting any swift gesture on his part to bring quick fire from the men who had ridden up with Bryan Hall.

He drew his gun, and watched the young Dailys press up behind Porine, and sent his low voiced warning and saw their heads come around, and the fury grow quickly in their lean faces.

"Don't do it."

They sat motionless, as if the snow which blanketed their horses' feet had sent up enough chill to freeze them solid. Motionless, but watchful, ready to take a hand at the first break which offered.

They were in a little island, as if withdrawn from the men who had come out with Hall. This group were circled about the two men who still struggled in the snow, paying no attention to the side play between the Dailys and Porine, as if they realized that this was not the main show.

Cantwine's quiet voice reached Porine. "Get Daily's gun."

Porine had been sitting motionless, his back to Cantwine, not knowing exactly what was happening behind him and not daring to turn his head.

Cantwine's words were like a reprieve. The smile was back on his crooked mouth and he used his free hand to reach across and lift the old man's gun from its holster. Then he backed his horse until he had the Daily boys before him, feeling utterly confident now of handling the situation, hoping against hope that one of the boys would start something.

The Dailys were furious, but old Pete was more concerned with retrieving his cows than with a fight. He ignored his sons. He ignored the fact that Porine still had his gun. He thrust his horse forward into the circle of mounted men that surrounded the fighters.

As he did so, Tolliver broke free of Hall's grasp and came up to his feet. He stood there for an instant trying to wipe the snow which was half blinding him from his eyes, then as Hall charged he set himself and drove two blows, a left, then a right to Hall's chin.

The banker went down. He lay for an instant on his back, then rolled over slowly and managed to lift himself with his hands until he was almost to his knees. Suddenly his arms went slack under him and he fell forward onto his face.

Karl Zeeman was out of his saddle at once, lifting the banker, saying to the swaying Tolliver, "That's enough,

Owen. That's enough. You whipped him."

His quick action kept the fight from spreading fur- ther. Owen Tolliver knew that. His own arms were leaden. He doubted if he could have managed another blow if he'd had to, but there was no satisfaction in him, no pleasure of victory. He had licked Bryan Hall with his fists, but it would take more than fists, far more, to lick these men who sat facing him. He had won but he had also lost. He knew it, without hearing Pete Daily's voice, without listening to the angry grumble of the assembled men.

He turned and walked stiffly to his horse. Ray Cantwine had caught it and was holding the animal at the side. Cantwine said in a low voice,

"Need help?"

Owen Tolliver was not certain that he could lift his battered body into the saddle, but he was not about to accept help in the presence of these men. He caught the horn with both hands, got his foot into the stirrup, and somehow managed to boost himself up.

Bryan Hall was not in such good shape. Two other men had joined Zeeman on the ground, one steadied the banker while the other wiped off his puffy face with snow.

Tolliver stared down at the man, feeling that Hall was the cause of most of his trouble. Without Hall to furnish the leadership these men would not have stood against him.

He had whipped Hall with his fists, but he had not whipped the determination out of him. Hall was fast recovering and as long as Hall was there these ranchers would stand together, demanding that he return their cattle. He knew this even before Pete Daily pressed his horse forward, followed by his angry sons.

"Well, Owen?"

Tolliver glanced toward where Zeeman was just remounting his horse. He met the marshal's eyes and saw Zeeman shake his head. He had a great respect for Zeeman's shrewdness. He felt that actually the marshal was on his side, and that Zeeman knew that the cause was lost.

He said, steadily, "All right, Pete. Nothing much in this world is settled by fighting. I suppose I had no right to force you to do something which in your own heart you know you should do. Here's your bill of sale."

He reached into his pocket, careful that his motion would not be misunderstood, and drew out the papers he had had the ranchers sign. He found Daily's and thrust it into the old man's hand.

Daily stared down at it, hating the paper, and the man who had made him sign it, and the part he was playing in all this.

But Owen Tolliver was paying no attention to him. He pushed his horse sidewise until he was before Grover. The smaller rancher refused to meet his eyes as he reached out to take back his bill of sale.

Afterward Tolliver repeated the process as he handed Turner his paper and then the rest. He stopped for a moment, holding in his hand the bill of sale that Ray Cantwine had given him, and then kneed his horse over to Cantwine's side.

Porine was sitting there, at ease in his saddle, his face a little mocking as he watched the grouped men. He looked at Tolliver, saying in a neutral voice,

"Say the word and we'll drive these cattle through them."

Tolliver knew that Porine did not mean it. Porine realized as he realized that what they had attempted was now hopeless.

Silently he extended the bill of sale toward Cantwine saying in an emotionless voice, "I guess I won't be needing your cows after all."

Cantwine looked at him. He turned his eyes to range across the men behind Bryan Hall with a certain deliberate arrogance, and when he spoke his words carried clearly to the farthest rider.

"Keep them."

Owen Tolliver stared at him.

Cantwine was saying, "A lot of people in this valley have doubted my word in the past, and I did not care because my opinion of them is no higher than their opinion of me. But no matter what they think, when I once sign an agreement I stand by it. Keep the cows. They aren't mine any longer."

He stared at Tolliver as if daring him to argue, then he pulled his horse around and paraded across before the semi-circle of watching men, sneering at them, daring them to pick up his words, to re-establish the fight.

They watched him wordlessly, not one of them accepting the unvoiced challenge and he rode on around the herd, motioning for his brother to join him. Together they pulled away, not once looking back.

Karl Zeeman let his breath escape with an audible rush. The marshal had not realized that he had been holding it, but the marshal was a trained fighting man, and he knew, more certainly than anyone else present, that only by the sheerest luck general bloodshed had been averted this day.

Nor was the danger entirely passed. Porine sat watchful, his hand still on his gun, the two Daily boys staring at him in sullen anger.

And Bryan Hall, as his strength flowed back into his big body, was sullen and dangerous. True, he had won over Tolliver in that the Box M foreman had returned the bills of sale, but he had taken a licking at Tolliver's hands before half of the ranchers in the valley, and the knowledge burned into him with the vitriolic fire of distilled wormwood.

He sat, watching Tolliver through angry eyes, trying to think of an excuse to renew the argument. But Pete Daily wanted no further trouble. He had his cows safe, and the quicker they were returned to his own pasture the happier he would be. He motioned to his sons, and after a reluctant look at Porine they pulled away and began cutting their animals from the herd. Their movement acted like a signal, and the rest of the ranchers moved in to help.

For a moment Bryan Hall hesitated, then he joined

them, riding past Tolliver without even looking at him. Zeeman pushed his horse up until he was close to Tolliver and Porine and the three sat silent, watching as the herd was broken into small bunches and the owners started their charges on the road for home.

"You almost got away with it," he said.

Tolliver turned hot eyes upon him. "No help from you."

Zeeman said, evenly, "A man who enforces the law must live by the law, Owen, otherwise we cease to have any law."

Porine laughed. His respect for the law was thin indeed.

Zeeman looked at him. "There could have been shooting." His tone was mild, reproving. "Would that have proved anything, or would it have helped those Indians?"

Porine cared nothing about the Indians. He pulled his horse around with a muttered curse and rode back to join Mac. Zeeman watched him go.

"A dangerous man."

"Sometimes," said Tolliver, rubbing his bruised cheek, "I can understand exactly how he feels."

Zeeman nodded. "We all can." He turned his head and it was he who first saw Grace Perkins riding toward them. For a minute he did not know who she was, then he realized and frowned deeply.

This, the marshal felt, was becoming too deeply involved. The bad blood already between Tolliver and Bryan Hall needed no added reason for hatred.

He sighed. In Joe John's time there had been little strife among the valley people, and few outsiders to stir up trouble. But it was not his place to say anything and Tolliver was not conscious of the girl's approach until she had nearly reached them. Then he turned and seeing her rode forward in surprise.

"Grace, what are you doing here?"

She was staring at his battered face. She saw the ranchers moving the cattle out and realized that the showdown had already come and passed.

"You're all right?"

He said, "Of course," and then realized why she was here and looked at her with renewed warmth. "As all right as a man can be who has failed to do what he started to."

She said, "I'm a fool I guess. My mother told me not to mix into men's affairs, but I was in the bank when Grover came to get Bryan, and the men with him were all armed."

"And you rode out to help me?" He had not recovered entirely from his surprise.

"I had to," she said, and unwrapped the scarf which had covered the lower part of her face. "I didn't know what I meant to do, but I couldn't stay quietly in town."

"Why, thank you for coming." He was held by an odd embarrassment, by the awareness that it was this girl rather than Martha who had ridden to his aid.

"And they took the cattle?"

He turned to look. Already the herd had been broken

up. The Dailys had started their beef for home. The others were preparing to follow, and Bryan Hall and the northern ranchers had pulled to one side.

Only Cantwine's animals remained in the trampled patch where the herd had been, twenty head, bewildered. He raised his hand, waving at Mac and Porine.

They understood the gesture and moved in, bunching the Cantwine cattle and starting them toward the Box M.

Bryan Hall had turned and seen the girl. For a moment he sat his horse, motionless, fresh anger rising up through him. Then he dug his spurs into the animal's sides and came forward, saying harshly before he reached them, "Grace, what are you doing here?"

She saw the bruises on his face, and remembered the marks on Tolliver's cheeks, and knew exactly what had happened as if the fight had been described for her, and her voice was level and without emotion as she said,

"I rode out to watch your triumph."

He flushed angrily. It was all he could do to control himself, to say in a biting tone, "That was very foolish, in this weather."

She was not cowed by his manner and his obvious displeasure. "At times," she told him, sharply, "I enjoy doing foolish things, but I can't say that I approve of what you have done here this afternoon."

He did not answer her directly. Instead he threw an angry look at Tolliver, saying sharply, "I've got to get you back to town. There's going to be more snow."

"I came alone," she was unyielding. "I can return the same way."

"I'll see you home," Owen Tolliver said.

For a moment the watching Zeeman thought that the banker meant to drive his horse against Tolliver's and so renew their fight, and he reached out, grasping Hall's bridle rein and urging his own mount ahead, saying in a quick, sharp undertone,

"Stop it, Bryan. The girl is free to ride with whom she wishes."

Bryan Hall was furious. "Karl, keep out of this."

"No," said Zeeman. "I always thought that you had a cool head. I doubt it now."

The words reached Hall as no other words might have done. For years he had prided himself on his cool control, on the fact that he seldom showed his true personal feelings to anyone.

He was still angry, but he knew that he would gain nothing by further fighting with Tolliver at the moment. With an angry gesture he wrenched his bridle rein free and spurring his horse headed up the tracked roadway toward the distant town. For an instant Zeeman hesitated, then he followed. The northern ranchers, seeing their leader spur away, put their own mounts into motion. They rode past Tolliver and the girl without a single sidewise glance.

As they pulled away Grace said, "Those men were your friends, Owen. You'll miss them."

He shrugged. Mac and Porine already had the Cantwine cattle started toward the Box M and it was time to go. They rode together toward Benton, the wind making conversation difficult. The snow caught them before they had covered half the distance, and they were forced to fight the horses to keep them headed into the blizzard.

Above the rush of the wind he shouted, "Maybe we'd better stop at Zeigler's. If it gets dark we're liable to lose the road."

She shook her head. "Not if we can make it. Mother will be worried if I don't come in."

He said, "It's only five miles, we can try," and they pushed on, the cold increasing, the wind seeming to jerk the breath from their bodies before they could inhale. It was the sixth straight day of the storm. It did not seem possible that it could continue much longer.

CHAPTER 9

BRYAN HALL watched Tolliver and the girl ride in an hour after nightfall. He had been in town less than thirty minutes himself, and the cold had not yet been sucked from his body, but quick anger at sight of them rose up through him.

It was characteristic that Bryan Hall stopped first at the bank, to check on the record of the day's business before he thought of his personal comfort. But all thought of business was driven from his mind as he stood at the bank window, the room dark behind him, and watched Tolliver escort Grace Perkins from the livery to the restaurant.

His impulse was to dash out and confront Tolliver, but twice within the last twenty-four hours he had given way to an impulse of violence and both times he could hardly have been classed the winner.

He schooled himself to watch, to wait. He expected to see Tolliver come from the restaurant and continue on to the hotel. Certainly Tolliver would have to report his failure to Martha Martel, and the thought brought Bryan Hall a certain pleasure.

But the seconds stretched into minutes and the minutes into almost an hour, and he began to fret. What was keeping Tolliver at the restaurant?

He curbed his curiosity and lit a cigar, puffing on it slowly as he always did to conserve the burning aroma as long as possible, but the tight wrapped leaves had turned to ash, and he had thrown away the short butt long before Tolliver reappeared, not turning toward the hotel as Hall expected, but heading back for the livery.

Tolliver had had no idea that he was being watched. He had enjoyed his dinner, sitting calm and relaxed in the warm kitchen of the restaurant, feeling more at home than he had anywhere since Joe John's death.

Some of the sting of his defeat at the hands of the ranchers was washing away, and the coldness which had numbed his big body and made the bruises on his face ache was vanishing.

Mrs. Perkins set the food on the big scrubbed table and then came to sit with them, saying, "A person is a fool to stay in this country. In south Texas, when I was a girl we seldom saw snow."

"Depends on what part of the state you mean," Tolliver was recalling Joe John's stories of the Staked Plains, of the blue northers which swept across the flat country with such startling suddenness.

"I've heard of cattle freezing on the hoof, of standing for days, like statues cut out of stone, and yet dead. At least we have some shelter here in the valley. The hills cut off a part of the wind and the stock can't drift much over fifty miles in any direction."

He pushed his coffee cup away with a satisfied sigh and his hand went unconsciously toward his shirt pocket, and Mrs. Perkins said, understandingly, "Smoke if you wish."

His eyes thanked her. He lit the cigar and drew deeply upon it, thinking how warm and comfortable it was here, and dreading the ride to the ranch.

Outside the wind rattled and the snow drove against the metal roof with a sound like hail, and he heard Mrs. Perkins say, "I hope it stops soon. It sure isn't good for business. I haven't had four customers since noon."

He thought about her words, wondering where the men who had ridden with Bryan Hall had eaten. Perhaps at the hotel, or more likely they had pressed on for home in spite of the storm.

But no matter where they had gone they had succeeded in their purpose. They had taken back the cows, and robbed him of the slightest chance of gathering a herd from the ranchers.

He realized that his mind was wandering, that Grace and her mother were talking about the Indians and that he had not been paying attention.

Grace was saying, "We might pack a couple of sleds with food and send them up over the pass."

Watching her he thought, out of all the people in the valley she is one of the few who are worrying about the starving people. She's trying to help, but what she is suggesting wouldn't do much good.

Aloud he said, "All the food in this valley wouldn't do any real good, and with this snow there isn't much chance of hauling in more. To all intents we're snow-bound, and the way the snow is piling up it won't melt out of the northern pass before May. Those Indians need meat, beef on the hoof which can be slaughtered and used as the time comes. That's the only way they will get through the winter."

Grace was staring at him, a hopeless look in her eyes. "But none of the ranchers will send their cows and you haven't the money to buy stock. I have nearly two hundred dollars. It isn't much. I was saving it against my wedding." Her cheeks were brighter suddenly, and the added color did not come from the heat. "Maybe if we took that and bought twenty head others would fall in line."

He did not tell her that twenty head would do no good, or that no matter what she did the people of the valley were not going to offer any help.

You could not disparage a gift when the donor was offering everything that she had. But her words gave him a renewal of courage. He had felt before that he was fighting alone, helplessly alone. Now at least one person had offered assistance and his voice was gentle when he said,

"Thank you, Grace, but your money won't be necessary. Save it for your proper send-off into married life. I'll get the cattle we need."

She was startled into looking at him quickly. "Get them, but where?"

There was only one answer and he wondered now why he had not realized it from the start. It was what Joe John would have wanted him to do, what Joe John would have done without a moment's hesitation had he still been alive.

"From the Box M," he said.

Grace could not conceal her surprise. "Will Martha let you?"

"I won't tell her," he said. "Not until the herd is gathered, not until it's too late for her to refuse."

"Owen, you can't do that. It isn't fair to her."

Deliberately he ground out his cigar butt in the saucer of his coffee cup. "Martha isn't going to be pleased," he said. "But it's something that has to be done, and in a way it's her fault that I have to do it."

"But to take her cattle . . . without telling her."

"The cattle were Joe John's. It is the way he would want it."

Grace was torn by her knowledge of the Indians' desperate need and her feeling of outrage for the other girl. "Don't do it, Owen, not this way. If a man pulled a trick like that on me I'd never speak to him again as long as I lived."

"A man would never have to trick you, Grace."

Her cheeks were very bright, but she held her voice steady. "Give Martha a chance, a chance to do the right thing without being forced."

He picked up his coat and was struggling into it, and the note of bitterness in his tone showed how deeply Martha's action of the night before had hurt him.

"I gave her her chance. Thanks for the supper and goodnight." He was gone then, without a backward glance and Mrs. Perkins saw tears in her daughter's eyes as the outer door slammed.

Grace said, slowly, "I've got to tell her."

Her mother's voice was sharp. "You'll tell no one. It is not your business."

"But she'll never forgive him."

Mrs. Perkins thought that it would be better for everyone if Martha Martel did not forgive him, but she held her words and turned toward the sink.

Tolliver was moving quickly past the bank and on down the snowy street. Bryan Hall watched him turn into the livery with narrowed eyes, then saw him reappear, mounted, and ride off south. Suddenly Hall's anger was gone and he felt pleased with himself and with the way things were happening. As far as the ranchers were concerned, Tolliver was beaten. It only remained to discredit him with Martha.

With this in mind he left the bank quickly, walking rapidly through the snow to the hotel. He entered the lobby to find her seated in one of the cane-backed chairs, and guessed that she knew that Tolliver was in town and was waiting to see him, and smiled to himself, saying,

"It's over. Owen failed to gather a herd."

She said, "I know. Some of the ranchers were here for supper. They were polite, but I could tell that they thought the Box M was whipped."

He looked at her sharply in surprise, hearing the hurt pride in her tone. "I thought that was what you wanted, the cows kept in the valley?"

"Of course, but the Box M has been the leading outfit here for a long time."

He said, carefully, "It wasn't the Box M that got whipped today. It was Owen Tolliver."

She said, "I'll tell Owen that as soon as he comes."

Bryan Hall took a deep breath. "He isn't coming, Martha. He rode in with Grace Perkins an hour ago and went to the restaurant. He rode south ten minutes ago."

She stared at him, wordlessly, and he said, softly, "It's time to take some action, Martha. It's time to show the valley that Owen Tolliver and the Box M are not the same thing."

CHAPTER 10

THE BUNKHOUSE WAS DARK when Owen Tolliver came into the ranch yard, and the place as silent as if the crew had smothered in the piled up snow.

He turned his horse into the barn and hesitated, wondering if there was a fire burning in the main house. He was so thoroughly chilled that he doubted if he would ever be warm again, and at the instant did not care.

He picked up a couple of blankets from the tack room and made his painful way across to the bunk-shack, pushing open the door. The gust of over-heated air burned against his frosted cheeks, and the eye of the stove door gave him enough light to find the empty bunk. He rolled into it, wrapping the blankets around him, not even shedding his coat, and lay on the lumpiness of the straw tick, not moving as the room's warmth crept through him.

Finally he rose, pulled off the coat and his boots and rearranged the blankets on the bunk, then he was asleep, as suddenly as if he had struck his head on a stone wall.

He came awake slowly, groggily, hearing the sound of moving men, hearing the murmur of their voices without associating it with words. He opened his eyes finally to see Porine standing over him, fully dressed, his unshaven cheeks showing the little frost lines put there the previous day, like interlacing veins turned purple.

Porine said, speaking clearly for everyone to hear, "Never mind the shovels, boys, he's alive after all."

Tolliver threw back the blankets and sat up, cursing as he did so at his stiffness. He got his feet upon the floor and ran his fingers comb-like through his tangled hair. "Is it still snowing?"

Porine looked at Mac and shook his head. "The man has lost his mind. Is it snowing, he asks, as if it could do anything else in this blasted country. It isn't. It stopped an hour ago, but from the looks of the sky it could start again, any time."

Tolliver heaved himself up from the bunk, reaching for the boots he had hurled toward the stove. They had dried, twisted and stiff and he had real trouble working his feet into them.

He stood up then and walked over to the washbench which had been moved inside, and dipped heated water from the bucket on the stove top, and washed his face and hands, coming more alive.

He was conscious that the three men watched him, a question in their eyes, but he did not speak, getting his coat and leading the way across the white yard to the cookshack and breakfast.

They ate like men turned ravenous by starvation, for in this weather their bodies burned up energy rapidly and Tolliver did not speak until he had finished his third cup of coffee and thrust away his plate.

Then he said, "We're taking eight hundred Box M steers over the pass, and from the looks of the weather the quicker we get moving the more apt we are to get there."

They regarded him, their eyes reserved, their thoughts indrawn and considering, and he knew a moment of hopeless bafflement. What if they refused to ride with him? What if they refused to risk their necks in such a venture?

He could not make them go. No man had the right to ask a crew, any crew to undertake such a thing.

But Porine was saying to Shorty, "What did I tell you? Didn't I say that Owen wasn't licked?"

Owen Tolliver felt that he had never heard sweeter words from anyone. He was on his feet, laughing at them, saying in a voice which had lost its tiredness, "When did a little snow ever lick anyone?"

He outlined his plans then, the plans he had made last night during the long ride home. He said, "We'll have no trouble bringing up the stock. Most of the steers are around the ricks below the creek."

Shorty said, slowly, "It will take all the beef stock we have."

Owen grinned at him. "What matter? They're long twos and some threes. We'll have less to bother with next fall. When the valley hears that I got ten dollars a head in gold they'll wish they'd joined in the drive. We'll take two spare horses apiece and extra teams for the sled. We'll stop at ranches every night until we reach the mouth of the pass, and we'll buy hay where we stop."

Porine's eyes lighted. "What if they won't sell you hay?"

Tolliver did not answer him. He merely looked, and all of them in the room knew what he meant.

"We'll make it," he said. "It's seventy-two miles by the trail from Benton to the agent's house. We'll only have the twenty-four miles through the pass without feed, and the Indians will meet us below the Devil's Cut and help us through. We'll make it." He turned to give the cook his orders then, how many blankets each man should have, extra clothing, extra boots. He was leaving no more to chance than he could help.

But when they went out after the stock the depth of the snow gave him pause. It was noticeably deeper than it had been on the day before, coming in places almost to the cattle's bellies. His horse floundered, struggling in the drifts, but on the lower bedground it was so trampled that it was easy to round up the animals they wanted, driving them through the gate of the big corral past the cook, perched on the top pole, an old stocking cap over his ears, his twisted fingers tallying the steers as they passed.

They milled, bawling their displeasure, trying to circle back toward the hay in the feed lot, but Tolliver held them as Porine rode up saying, "What about that twenty head of Cantwine's in the small corral?"

"Throw them in." Owen Tolliver did not really care. Yesterday those twenty steers had been important, because they represented the first gather from the ranchers, the starting plug he had hoped would move the whole valley to fall in line.

But his effort had failed, and now they were merely twenty head and since he was stripping the Box M of all beef stock, twenty animals one way or another made small difference. But there was no need to hurt Cantwine's pride. The bench rancher might have sent them unwillingly, but he had derived something from not taking back his bill of sale when all the others had demanded theirs, and he had paraded that pride in the mocking way he had ridden across before the others.

The twenty head were pushed after the rest and Owen glanced at his watch in satisfaction. They had worked quickly. It was barely eight o'clock and already Mac and Shorty were hazing the leaders out into the roadway. He made a quick estimate, eleven miles to town, call it twelve. He said to Porine, "Move them along. I'd like to make Benton by tonight."

The Irishman looked at him. "Pushing a little, aren't you?"

Owen Tolliver had his own reasons for wanting to make Benton that night, reasons which he had no intention of mentioning to Porine.

He said, "They're fresh. They haven't had much exercise in the last ten days. They'll step out for the first two or three miles, and after we pass Zeigler's the road is fairly well broken, been a lot of travel up that way. We'll make it easily if the snow holds off and the wind keeps down. The more distance we cover today the less we'll have tomorrow. Push them out."

As Porine rode to join Mac and Shorty, Tolliver turned back to give last instructions to the cook. "You drive the chuck sled as far as Benton," he said. "I'll hire someone there to drive it on, and you can come home to look after the calves and the she stock."

The cook spat against his hot stove and said in a disgruntled voice, "Twenty-three roundups I've cooked for this crew. I guess I'm not too old to take a ride in the snow. Hire someone else to come out and care for the stock."

Tolliver looked at him. The man was old. It was on

the tip of Owen's tongue to point out that they would have trouble enough without an old cook to worry about. But he didn't. This was the kind of loyalty he understood, the pride of belonging to an outfit, of riding with that outfit no matter what it cost. How could he tell a man like that that he was too old?

He nodded then and went out and drove the spare horses from the holding corral into the broad path that the slow moving cattle had made. He had little fear that the horses would try to stray. He motioned for Shorty to drop back with the drag and himself took the point with Mac and Porine on the opposite flanks.

It was hard work, gruelling work. They needed more hands and he racked his brains, trying to think of a spare rider anywhere. There were seldom any unattached hands in the valley. On other ranges there were always stray cowboys, passing the winter on the grubline, but the valley outfits were all small, and seldom hired outside men.

And then, far off to the east he saw three men riding toward him, angling across the uneven white surface of the valley, and wondered who they were and did not guess until they were less than half a mile from him.

They rode up, coming out of the side track which led back to Sunken Wells, and Ray Cantwine reined in beside him, saying with his trace of mockery, "Hiring any hands, Mr. Tolliver?"

Owen Tolliver said cautiously, "Come back for your twenty steers?"

Cantwine laughed. "You'd insult the devil himself if

he offered you aid."

"I couldn't be more surprised," Tolliver told him. "What are you after, Ray?"

Cantwine said, "Why, you're smart, Owen. You can figure things out. We've come to steal all your cattle. We're going to drive them over the next rise and hide them in a snow drift until spring. Use your head, man. Take what help you can get, even if it has a bad name."

"I'll take it," said Tolliver. "I was merely curious."

For an instant he thought Cantwine did not mean to answer, then the man said, "Maybe I've been hungry, Friend Owen. Maybe I know what it is to have nothing to stick to your ribs. I make no pretense of loving Indians, but, when I'm snug in my shack, eating Box M beef, I'd hate to think of the warwhoops not having any."

Tolliver did not answer.

"So I brought Charley and the Mex along, thinking maybe you could use some extra hands."

"I can. I was wondering who I could hire in town."

"No one," said Cantwine. "After what happened yesterday who would ride with you?"

"What about your own stock?"

Cantwine shrugged. "We hazed them over to Grover's before daylight. I told him I'd break his scrawny neck if one of them dies."

Tolliver was staring at him. "Before daylight? How'd you know I intended to make this drive? I was hardly certain myself."

Cantwine showed him a thin smile before he raised

the neck-cloth to protect his lower face. "A man like me has to know the people who live around him, Owen. I probably know you better than you know yourself. You're too stubborn to quit at anything, once you think that you are right. You had to drive these steers. You promised that Indian you would, and they'll be waiting up there in the pass, hungry. It's something you have to do because if you don't you'd never rest for the remainder of your life. You'd have Joe John's ghost prodding you, every time you hit the bunk."

He waved then and rode to the side, speaking to his brother and the Mexican. They dropped back to help with the drag.

CHAPTER 11

THEY REACHED ZEIGLER'S before noon, making better time than even Owen had dared hope for. The cook had caught them with his sled and Owen put it out in front, its double team and heavy runners serving as a kind of plow to break the piled snow for the plodding cattle.

The herd was strung out a good quarter of a mile, and three men came out into Zeigler's yard to watch them pass, but none called a greeting, and none rode out to help.

Tolliver thought bitterly that the rift was even deeper than he had realized. A week ago, Zeigler and his two hands would have fallen in with them merely for the sake of being neighborly. But now, every action he took would be viewed with quick suspicion by all.

He raised his hand as he rode past the gate, and got no gesture in return, and heard Cantwine who was riding near him say with snide satisfaction, "You know now how it feels to be an outcast, Friend Owen. You know how I have felt for years."

Tolliver realized that what the man said was true. Each time Cantwine had ridden into a yard he had been greeted with reserved suspicion which must have been harder to bear than outright threats. He did not answer, for there was no real answer to give. He pushed on, not calling a noon halt for they were still nearly six miles short of town.

But at least the snow had held off, and he began to hope that perhaps the worst of the storm had passed, but there were still lowering clouds in the west.

The clouds though were better than a glaring sun reflected off the glittering snow. He was beginning to hate snow. He had never felt this way about winter before. Winter usually meant a chance to rest, to repair gear, to sit beside the fire, to venture out only often enough to feed the stock.

But in his full memory there had never been such a winter in the valley. Theirs was a sheltered place, and the snow seldom lingered on the ground for more than a few weeks at a time. And even with snow, the wind normally swept patches of bunch grass clear so that the animals found some graze in all of the winter months.

But this fall had been different. One snow had piled

upon another and they had already received more than their annual pack, and it was not yet Christmas.

He had forgotten all about Christmas. Christmas was only a few days away and the valley had always made a big thing of Christmas. There would be a party at the hotel, and a dance on New Year's, and much visiting. He wondered if he would be back in time, and then he realized that he would no longer be welcome.

This came as something of a new thought. He had not looked ahead at the future. He had thought of this trouble as only a passing thing, which, when the drive was accomplished, would be quickly forgotten. But now he knew that the enmities he had stirred up ran deep, and that if he were successful in pushing the herd over the pass, that very act would be held against him. Martha would forgive him if he were successful, because she would share in that success, but the rest of the valley would not.

Unconsciously he quickened the pace. He had to get to Benton. News of their approach would soon be carried to the town, and Martha would guess whose cattle he drove.

He wanted to talk to her before she had the chance to say something which she would afterward regret. But he could not push ahead alone as yet, not at least until the town was well in sight.

And the afternoon was passing with disturbing rapidity, the cattle slowing, more inclined to attempt to turn out of the roadway, to want to lie down.

And the clouds were alarmingly lower. It was going

to start snowing again soon, the feel of it was in the air.

He thanked God for the Cantwines. Whatever else they were, they were born cowmen. Charley especially had a quieting way with the animals, ranging backward and forward along the slowly moving herd, his very presence calming them, moving them forward.

And the Mexican was handling the horses. Tolliver did not know what the man's name was. Perhaps the name had been purposely forgotten, left behind him as so many other men in this country had buried their identity, seeking security by being nameless, almost faceless. You did not ask a man his name. You accepted him for what he claimed to be until circumstances pointed to the error of such a course.

They climbed a slight rise and Benton's buildings appeared, hard to see, blending almost perfectly into the whiteness around them with their snow laden roofs. The early night was already darkening, hastened by the heavy cloud bank which obscured the setting sun.

A light sparkled from the town ahead as if some enterprising merchant had lighted his lamps deliberately as a beacon to the tiring men, and Tolliver used it as a signal to ride over to Porine's side, saying, "I'll push ahead and talk to Parkingstead about some hay. Throw them onto the flat place to the southwest of town. It's close to his stacks, and tell the cook to pull the sled into the livery corral."

He was gone then, kicking his tired horse into a half gallop, his eyes on the rutted road, picking the easiest path that he could find.

He came into the top of the main street and turned down it, pulling up before the livery, conscious that there was a small knot of men before the Star, and paying them no attention as he turned the tired animal into the barn and eased himself stiffly out of the saddle.

Parkingstead limped from the cluttered office, saying in a neutral tone, "You're getting to be my steadiest customer, Owen."

"I've got more business for you," Tolliver said as he pulled off the saddle with its ice encrusted stirrups. "I've got eight hundred hungry beeves headed your way. They'll make quite a hole in your stacks, Emil, but I'll pay."

Parkingstead's tone had sudden disapproval. "You'll pay what I ask, no more, no less. I guessed that you'd try to make town when I first heard of the drive. My hostler has been hauling hay to the flats all afternoon."

Tolliver was surprised. "You got the news so soon?" He had a sinking feeling of dismay. He was already too late. He had gained nothing by riding ahead, for Martha would have known about the drive for hours.

He thought about it as he left the barn. At least she had not gotten on a horse and ridden out to order him to turn around. He hoped that she realized there was no chance of turning back, that the decision had been taken, the Box M committed.

On the street he knew a sudden reluctance to face her, to listen to her reproaches, to see her anger, and he hesitated, remembering something he had forgotten, and turned in at the restaurant.

He came through the door, hoping that Mrs. Perkins would be alone, for he did not feel like talking to Grace either. But she was waiting on one of the front tables as he entered and he had no chance to avoid her.

She turned, hearing the door, and seeing him came quickly to meet him. He kept his voice impersonal, saying in a low tone, "I've got eight hungry men bringing in the herd. It will probably take a good hour to get the cattle settled and started to feed. Can you stay open long enough to serve us? Have you enough food?"

Mrs. Perkins had stepped from the kitchen, smiling. "Don't worry," she said. "As soon as the news came that you were on the road Grace ordered extra food. We've enough cooked to feed twenty hands."

The girl's cheeks had reddened, and she shot her mother a resentful glance, but Mrs. Perkins appeared not to see. She turned back into the kitchen, leaving them alone save for the three riders eating at the front table.

These had looked around at his entrance, but had now gone back to their meal as if they were afraid that he might speak to them.

Tolliver had no intention of doing so. He had in fact hardly noticed who they were, and he had no interest. "Thank you," he said. "We're probably hungry enough to eat for twenty. We did not stop at noon."

Her eyes were on his face, and her color had dulled as she recovered her control. "Did you have much trouble?"

"It went too easily," he told her. "It was so easy that it worries me. The snow held off, the road was fairly broken and the animals were fresh. Tomorrow may be different, and the farther north we get, the worse it's apt to be."

"But you'll make it?"

He looked at her intently. "Do you believe I'd try it if I didn't think there was a fair chance of getting through?"

She nodded. "I believe you would."

"Meaning I'm a fool?"

"No," she told him. "Not a fool. Stubborn maybe, but not a fool. Some things are worth a gamble, even when the odds are weighted against you."

His tone was short, "You weren't saying that last night."

Her color was coming up again. "Owen, have you seen Martha?"

This was the reason he had not wanted to talk to Grace at the moment. He had been afraid that she would return to the subject of Martha.

"Not yet."

"It was a cruel thing you did to her today. A dozen people have rushed to the hotel to tell her about the herd. I only hope she forgives you."

She turned then, and went into the kitchen. For a moment he did not move, then he lifted the sheep-skin collar of his coat and went into the night.

It was starting to snow again, scattered pellets turned icy-hard by the increasing cold. He felt them on his face as he came from the restaurant, and on the backs of his ungloved hands. He turned to look south, hoping to see the herd come into sight, but the darkness and the snow flurries hid his view.

He debated. If the storm increased they would need his help to bed the herd, but the wind was not noticeably higher, and the snow was still light. He crossed the rutted street instead and came into the familiar saloon with its welcome warmth.

There were half a dozen men at the bar and two card games going at the rear tables. Curly saw him enter. Curly set a glass upon the bar and he could not ignore it. Discourtesy was not a part of Owen Tolliver's nature, and he experienced a sudden, warm feeling for the nearly hairless bartender as Curly poured the whiskey, added sugar and then the steaming water with the bit of cinnamon.

It was a small thing, an act performed automatically for every rider who came in out of the chill, but it was the first time Owen Tolliver had been treated in a normal manner by anyone in this town during the last two days.

He raised the glass in silent toast to the bartender, and noticed that the others at the counter were watching him in the back mirror without turning to offer the usual greetings. He passed them, carrying the steaming glass and moved to the rear, stopping beside the card table at which Bryan Hall was seated.

He waited until the hand was played, and Tom Brenn raked in the pot, and then said in his even tone, "See you a minute, Bryan?"

Hall took his time to lift his eyes, as if he had not been conscious of Tolliver's presence in the room, offering no greeting, saying shortly, "Later, Owen. I'm busy now."

Owen Tolliver sipped his drink, knowing that Hall was watching, knowing that everyone in the room was watching and that they all expected trouble. And suddenly he was filled with a hot desire to satisfy them, to reach out and jerk the sitting man to his feet and drive his fist into Hall's slightly mocking face.

He schooled himself with difficulty, saying in a tightened voice, "This is business, otherwise I wouldn't bother to speak to you."

Curiosity sparked in Hall's eyes in spite of his certainness that the game was fully in his hands, and the room was so quiet that a piece of wood, cracking in the stove, was plainly audible.

He said, evenly, "I wasn't conscious that you and I still had any business, Owen."

"You have some money of mine in the bank," Tolliver said. "I'd like three hundred of it, in gold, tonight."

Hall's lips tightened. "The bank will be open for business as usual at nine o'clock tomorrow morning."

"By nine," said Tolliver, "I'll have the herd three miles north of town, and I'm not riding back for any banking. You've opened the bank after hours for less reason before."

Hall picked up the cards without looking at them,

and his quick fingers riffled the deck. He knew this conversation would be repeated over town and was savoring his small moment of triumph. "At my pleasure, yes. Why should you need your money now, Owen? It will be waiting here for you when you get back, if you get back."

This was the question which Tolliver had been waiting for the banker to ask, his real purpose for the conversation, and he raised his tone a trifle to be absolutely certain that everyone heard him clearly.

"I need it for hay," he said. "I mean to keep as much tallow on those beeves as I can. I'll buy hay all the way up to the pass, and with the lack of cooperation I've been getting, I figure that no one will take my promise to pay, that they'll want gold."

Hall was watching him. All the others were looking at him. Owen Tolliver's face was set, and there was a tight look about his eyes that warned them of danger.

This was his defiance to the valley, his warning to the northern ranchers that he expected hay from their places. The word would precede him up the trail. He knew it, wanted it to. He waited then until Hall said,

"Just write them an order. Everyone in the valley will honor an order on the bank."

"Will they?" said Tolliver. "I doubt it. From the way they've acted recently they wouldn't trust their own grandmothers. I want gold to pay them as I take the hay. You'd better get it for me, Bryan. Don't forget, I'm still chairman of the bank board. As such I have a key to the door, and one to the safe. If you don't want me messing up your carefully arranged accounts you'd better come over and get me the money."

Hall stared up at him, his smile gone. Then with a muttered oath he threw the cards half across the room, scattering them in all directions as he came to his feet. He did not even understand his own sudden fury. It was in reality a bursting sense of futility. Every time he thought that he had Tolliver backed into a corner Owen managed to win somehow. He wondered as he rose if he had again made a mistake, if by some miracle Tolliver would get the herd through unharmed. He thought not. The Devil's Cut at the head of the pass must be nearly full of snow. With the best of luck Owen would still have to turn his weary animals around and hope to get them back to the nearest ranch before they starved.

His rage held as he stamped the length of the long room, and without bothering to pick up his coat, plowed his way across the street to the bank. He was chilled by the short walk and his hand trembled as he fitted the big key into the massive lock and let them into the still heated room.

But the sharp, penetrating bite of the outside cold had served to quench the hot edge of his anger, leaving him with a cold dull fury which was like a gnawing pain at the pit of his belly.

He moved over to the square safe, and used his key, and pulled open the cash drawer, counted out three hundred dollars, and made little piles of the stacked coins on the corner of his desk. Then he mechanically made out the withdrawal slip and watched in bitter silence as Tolliver signed it.

Even in anger he was methodical. He replaced the things in the safe, locked it and stood up, watching as Tolliver carelessly transferred the loose coins to his coat pockets.

"Owen," he said in his dry tone, "a piece of advice. You have cast a long shadow for some time. But that time is passed. When you have lost those cows, or by sheer luck delivered them, keep riding. There is nothing left for you in this valley. It will never be as it was again, believe me. You have lost your position and your friends, and you will not gain them back."

Tolliver gave him a long look, then a small smile. "That's the way your hope runs, isn't it, Bryan? Nothing for me here, nothing for me anywhere?" He turned then and quietly left the bank.

CHAPTER 12

THE SNOWFALL HAD INCREASED and with it the wind. He stood for a moment on the bank steps, hesitating, and then, instead of moving toward the hotel as he had planned he turned back toward the livery.

Just as he reached the barn entrance he heard the crunch of the sled and saw the old cook drive the four horse team from the curtain of swirling snow and pull past him into the barn runway.

He helped the man down, and helped strip the harness from the winded horses, listening as the cook told him, "They're bunching them southwest of town. Someone already hauled hay to the flats."

He said, "Parkingstead did," and thanked the livery man mentally. He pondered whether he should offer pay from the gold in his pocket and decided against it. You insulted a man like Parkingstead by insisting on making payment before it was asked. At least the old man still remained his friend.

He got a fresh horse and saddled it and rode out to help the chilled men bed the animals down, and found that Porine and Ray Cantwine already had them milling quietly about the scattered hay piles, nosing at them tiredly, apparently oblivious to the wind and the driving snow.

"We'll be all right," Cantwine said, "unless the storm, gets worse and they start to drift."

"Tired as they are they won't drift far." It was Porine, and Owen Tolliver glanced at him.

The man was stiff with cold, and ice had formed across the arch of his eyebrows, under the low drawn brim of his whitened hat. Tolliver turned to ride slowly around the bedground, wondering as he had wondered before why a man like Porine endured the killing drive of the climate, the physical discomfort of the saddle work.

Porine was not the kind who put down deep roots, or felt the need. He was a drifter by both instinct and choice, a man who had ridden the land from one trail's end to another, a man whose only relaxation was a fight, a few drinks and perhaps a woman in some strange saloon.

And yet without question he had come along on this drive, hardly waiting for Owen's orders, working as hard as any of them. It was a contradiction in personality, an unfathomable something which made no sense when considered analytically. Porine, this man who now worked selflessly to get the cattle through, might well have stolen these same cattle if the opportunity had offered, if he had not been riding for the Box M, but say for Cantwine's outfit.

And the Cantwines, what were they doing here? They did not even owe him the slight loyalty that Porine did, yet he could not see where any of them stood a chance of self gain from this drive.

He puzzled over it as he completed his circle and came back to tell Porine, "Take the Cantwines and the Mex into the Perkins' restaurant. Some hot food will help. Mac and Shorty and I will wait until you get back. Then we'll take shifts, two at a time, the rest sleeping in the livery barn so that if trouble starts one can ride in to rout out the crew."

They rode away, vanishing where the snow curtain merged with the outlying houses of the town, and the world shut down around him, a world of bedded cattle and snow which hissed slightly as it fell through the night.

He moved slowly around the eating animals, watching as a steer raised its head, watching as some animal stirred unaccountably, disturbed by the dark reasoning of its lethargic mind.

A cow, he thought, was dumb. A cow would stand, head down, defying the world and all its works, but that same animal could become frightened inexplicably and transfer its senseless fear to a whole herd.

The wind was swirling about him now, the dropping temperature must be near the zero point. A miserable night, a dangerous night, a night which should be spent in a cheerful room beside a glowing stove, not in the saddle, nursing eight hundred half frozen cattle.

He passed Shorty, riding in the opposite circle and they did not speak. He came on around the herd, wondering how long the Cantwines and Porine had been gone and whether they would ever come back.

And finally they returned and in the heat of the restaurant he and Shorty and Mac were eating their delayed meal with deep relish. Mrs. Perkins waited on them, and Grace was not in the kitchen. He wondered if the girl was purposely avoiding him and put the thought from his mind as being silly. Why would she wish to avoid him? He missed her presence, but there were other people about, many others.

Even in the vicious weather they moved along the street, peering through the frosted windows as if he and his two riders had suddenly become members of some side-show troupe.

It was strange, he thought, how little it took to make a person an object for mass curiosity. Most of the townspeople had known him for years, but now that he had embarked on something which was opposed to the majority point of view he had become an unknown equation to be stared at with a touch of morbid fascination, and he sensed that as long as he remained in this valley men would remember him as the fool who had tried to drive a herd through the snow-choked pass.

It was his first real contact with spectators in the mass, and he found that he did not like being spied upon as if he were about to perform some astounding feat like suddenly sprouting a third eye.

His anger made him eat more rapidly and he finished first, neither Mac nor Shorty showing any consciousness that they realized that people were watching them.

He rose, gathering his coat from its hanging place against the wall and only pausing to say, "When you boys finish, ride out and take over the herd for the first hour. Tell the others to get some sleep and to keep out of the saloon. We'll do our drinking when we get back."

They stared up at him, letting their disappointment show, but they understood what he meant. They had watched enough barroom fights develop to understand. A chance word, a misunderstood phrase, a jibing remark, any of these could well lead to trouble when most of the riders in the valley were lined up on the other side.

He thanked Mrs. Perkins then, and asked her if she would have their breakfast ready an hour before daylight, and went out. People were still on the sidewalk, some of them before the restaurant, others across the street in front of the Star. He raked them with his eyes, feeling a hot intolerance, something akin to hate. He had the impulse to shout at them that if they lacked the courage to help at least they might have the decency not to stand and gawk.

But he schooled himself, turning toward the hotel, conscious that every eye on the street watched his progress, that everyone speculated on what he was about to say to the girl.

Martha was in the lobby. Martha did not rise from her cane-seated chair, and her face showed no pleasure as he moved toward her, but only a set grimness which he recognized as rage.

There were half a dozen people in the big room. Pop Caldwell loitered behind the high desk although he was usually to be found in the bar at this hour. Doctor Bemmis stood before him, pretending to talk.

Tolliver knew that it was only pretense. The gossipping old goat was worse than any woman. And Mrs. Fisk, the dressmaker, and her maiden daughter were on the far side of the room. Owen had never seen them in the hotel before.

He knew a feeling of utter frustration. Why couldn't these people mind their own business? Why on this night, of all nights must they concern themselves in his and Martha's affairs?

He crossed over to stand beside her chair, saying in a low, furious voice, "Whatever you do, smile, look glad to see me."

Her answering smile was an automatic thing. She was not, he realized, a finished actress, and she was very angry, but she did manage to say in a tone that was audible to everyone in the room, "I hope you didn't have too much trouble with the stock?"

"Not too much." He was as casual as if he drove eight hundred steers through belly-deep snow every day in the year. At least, he thought, she did not mean to create a scene before these people, but he had to talk to her, and alone. He said in a low tone, "I've got to speak to you, let's go up to your room."

He saw the quick disapproval in her eyes and thought with savage anger that she was more concerned with appearances than with having this out between them.

"It's better that way," his voice was a flat murmur. "The lesser of two evils. I won't keep you long."

She hesitated, but for a moment only. She had always been a person to make up her mind quickly. Without a word she rose and turning led the way toward the stairs. He followed, aware that conversation in the lobby had ceased and that every eye followed their progress. For himself it had little meaning, but he knew that Martha would keenly resent the gossip which this night would bring forth.

They climbed in silence, and he had to admire her poise. She might not be a good actress, but she was trying. They reached the upper hall and turned back along it to her room. She had the corner room, over-looking the town's street, the biggest room in the hotel, and she had dressed it to her own taste, bringing in items of furniture from the ranch.

He stood waiting while she unlocked the door, and

then struck a friction match and went past her to light the lamp which set on the bureau.

Afterward he turned to see that she had followed him, that she had closed the door. He did not have to wait then. Her attack was immediate and it came with all the vitriolic force which Joe John's daughter could put into words.

"I hope you are very proud of yourself."

He wasn't proud of himself, or of her, or of the sorry part the valley people had played in this business, and he told her so quickly, in no uncertain terms.

"You haven't played fair with me," he said. "Why didn't you object to sending the cattle when I first told you?"

"I did."

For an instant he was nonplussed, then he said, "But not flatly. You did not come out into the open to oppose me, you talked to Bryan Hall. You tried to hide behind the action of the other ranchers."

She said, quickly, "That's not entirely true and you know it."

"No," he was trying to keep his anger out of his voice, to be completely fair with her. "You're right, I knew when I first mentioned the Indians that you thought the idea foolish, but you didn't say so at the dance. You let others do the talking."

"And yet knowing how I felt, you went ahead."

"I thought I could make the other ranchers feel the need. I thought that they would fall in line."

"And you failed."

118

"And I failed."

"And then you were afraid to face me. You came into town last night, but you did not come near this hotel. You had already decided to steal my cattle, and you were afraid that if I talked with you I'd guess, I'd stop you."

That was true, he thought. He had been afraid to face her, but not quite in the way she meant. He had not wanted a direct showdown the night before. He had wanted to wait until the drive was under way, until the Box M was so committed to the project that even the girl would realize there was no turning back.

He said, "I didn't exactly steal your cattle."

"I don't know what else you call it." She made a visible effort to control her anger, but the toe under the hem of her dress was tapping dangerously. "Eight hundred head, almost all the beef stock the ranch has." Someone must have told her, he thought.

He said, measuring his words, "I didn't come up here to argue. Argument will get us nowhere."

"Then what did you come for?"

"To point out a few basic facts which I think you have overlooked. In the first place, you, along with everyone else have made up your minds that I can't get the herd through, that I'm driving them to certain death. I protest that. I'm going to get them through and I expect to be paid, well paid for every head."

A faint glimmer of hope came into her eyes. "You aren't just saying that? You honestly believe that you can get those cattle up through the pass?"

"With the Indians' help, yes. But that is not the only point. By your attitude you're forcing me to say something which I would rather not have had to mention. These cattle were Joe John's, and I'm driving them in an effort to keep a promise he made."

She moved her hands in an impatient gesture as if this was of no importance to her, but he went on.

"Do you remember last July when we first told Joe John that we'd decided to get married? He called us both in, and he pulled out a copy of his will, and he told us then that he had planned to change it, that he planned to leave half the stock to me and half to you, that you were to inherit the property with the understanding that I would stay and run the ranch for you and run my cattle with yours."

She did not answer. Her face had a tense, tight look which drained all the beauty from it.

Tolliver's voice was colorless as he went ahead. "And Joe John said that now we had decided to marry there was so need for him to alter the will, since what I had would be yours and what you had would be mine."

Still she did not speak.

"So, although the world may think I stole those steers, and apparently you so consider in your own mind, I don't. For what it is worth, my conscience is clear. I'm sorry this happened. I would rather it could have been in any other way, but there it is. I'll consider that if the stock is lost it was my share, given me by your father, lost in trying to discharge a debt which he would have wanted paid.

"If I get through the pass the money will belong to you, but we can't turn back. The Box M is committed to this drive. If we stopped now the valley would laugh at us for the rest of our lives."

Her voice was low, "You're right in that. Bryan Hall came here last night to tell me that people were already sneering at the ranch and to advise me to disassociate myself from you." She looked directly into his wind roughened face. "You knew that would happen when you brought those cattle into town without telling me. You knew that my pride in the ranch would force me to let you go on."

He nodded.

"I think I hate you." She said it slowly.

He showed no emotion. "Does that mean that you've decided not to marry me?"

She hesitated. "I'm not quite sure. I've got to think. But listen to me, Owen Tolliver. No matter what happens, whether I decide to marry you or not, don't ever do a thing like this to me again. Don't put me into a position of being forced to agree to something against my will."

CHAPTER 13

THEY BEGAN TO MOVE THE CATTLE OUT before daylight, driving the herd directly down the town's street. It would have been as easy to bypass Benton but some perverse impulse caused Tolliver to order the crew deliberately past the hotel.

They had breakfasted early, and as the chuck sled pulled opposite the restaurant Grace Perkins and her mother carried out cooked food in big hampers, passing them up to the old cook.

The crew was cheerful and rested and full of life, like small boys setting out on a pleasure jaunt. They hurrahed the cattle, their high, piercing yells waking the Benton citizens from their night's rest.

A crowd began to collect along the edge of the sidewalk. Porine and Ray Cantwine raced their horses back and forth along the side of the moving herd as if challenging the townsmen to try and block their progress.

Even Shorty and Mac caught the spirit, riding like madmen, breaking the lumbering animals into a slow trot. Karl Zeeman watched the antics with a disapproving eye, saying to Tolliver who sat his horse beside him,

"The fools, they'll stampede the whole lot."

Tolliver shrugged. "They won't run far. Let the boys warm up a little. They'll have small fun from here on north."

Zeeman looked at him. "Say the word and I'll go with you, Owen, although I'm not a great hand with cattle as you well know."

Tolliver said, "You're needed here, Karl. If you'll find a man to send out and care for my she stock, I'll be obliged."

"I'll go myself if I can't find anyone else."

Tolliver nodded and rode along the street to pause

122

before the restaurant, looking down into Grace's shawl-framed face. "That was nice of you, the cooked food I mean. It will save time and trouble."

"The least we could do." Her tone seemed short. "The best of luck, Owen."

"I'll need it," he said, and rode on, looking back from down the block to see her standing, motionless, watching him. Then he rode on to the hotel, noting that Martha's corner windows were dark and knew a momentary resentment that Martha had not cared enough to bother to see them off, and then he saw her step from the hotel doorway and rode to the edge of the gallery and bent in the saddle to kiss her, knowing that the whole town watched.

Her lips were stiff and cold and not responsive, and he rode away with the realization that he was glad to go. Something had happened between them in the last few days, a lack of the understanding that they had once shared so well.

The snow had stopped, and the sun came over the eastern mountains into a near clear sky, and its warmth brought the temperature gradually up, giving him hope that both the weather and their fortunes had changed.

The roadway had been marred by traffic, and even considering the occasional drifts the sled moved ahead behind its double team at gratifying speed. The cattle sensed the change in the weather and stepped out willingly, inclined to follow the confines of the road.

Porine was whistling as he rode up beside Tolliver, in better spirits than he had been for a full month. "Nearly like spring," he said. "Next thing we know it will turn slushy underfoot, and that fool Indian agent will decide winter is finished and he doesn't need our beef. Then we'll have to turn these critters around and trail them all the way back home again."

They were words Porine was to regret later that first day, for by midafternoon a new bank of clouds built up out of the west, cutting off the last rays of the sun so that it was near full dark as they pulled into the DeChute place.

They were tired by then, and their light spirits of the early morning were entirely gone. Porine especially seemed to be suffering from a let-down, turned sullen by the approach of the new storm.

Dutch DeChute met them in the, yard, and DeChute was not pleased to see them, a big, square man with massive hands and a slow way of speaking which brought his accented words out laboriously.

"So you want hay?"

Porine was out in front and he said, shortly, "We not only want hay, we intend to take it, Dutchy."

DeChute stared up at him, his heavy face seeming to redden in the last held daylight. "In this country you do not take a man's things, you ask for them."

"Do we?" said Porine. "Well then, we're asking for hay and taking it if you refuse."

Tolliver had heard this last as he rode up. He said, sharply, "Get back and bring up the horses."

Porine gave him a half resentful look, started to say something, changed his mind and swung his tired horse short around.

Tolliver had expected little trouble from DeChute, and he cursed Porine silently for the man's careless tongue. DeChute could be as stubborn as one of his bulls when his mind was set.

He told the big rancher, "Never mind Porine. We've had three bad days and his nerves are edgy. We need the hay, but you'll be well paid."

"Pay is it?" DeChute sounded more offended. "Such a way to talk with friends. The feed is short, that is what worries." He turned and motioned toward the stacks. "What you need, take," then he turned back into the house.

Tolliver was conscious of Porine's annoyance as they forked down the mountain hay. He said, "I know you're tired, but we're all tired so that's not much excuse."

There was something intemperate in Porine's manner. "I never saw a squarehead that I liked."

"Don't like him then," said Tolliver, "but remember that we still have a long way to go, and that we are driving cattle, not looking for a war."

Later as they ate in the big old fashioned kitchen with DeChute at the head of the scrubbed table he kept a sharp eye on Porine, but the Irishman held his silence, eating sullenly. When they were well finished DeChute brought out his huge china bowled pipe and packed the rough tobacco under a broad thumb and drew on it as a bellows sucks in air.

DeChute was not easy, nor was his big wife. He said

in a slow tone, "You are hating the valley, Owen, and the people in it because you feel that we've been heartless."

"Haven't you?" It was Porine, a light dancing suddenly in his wicked eyes.

Tolliver wanted to kick him under the table. DeChute, after a slow stare, ignored the Irishman. "We are not heartless," the big man said. "If those Indians came to this house they would be fed, even as you've been fed, but it's too much to ask that I ride in the snow, that I send cows on a trek which I know is foredoomed."

"No one's asking you to." It was Porine. "We've got enough trouble, Dutchy, without the likes of you."

Tolliver thrust back his chair. He wanted to get out of there before a real fight developed. He thanked the wife in a tone which over-rode the room and led the crew outside, saying angrily to Porine as they came out into the cold,

"We've enough trouble without you wearing a chip on your shoulder. If you've got so much energy you need a fight I'll work it out of you; take the first night trick."

Porine threw him an angry look and strode away after his horse. Ray Cantwine said, soberly, "You'll have trouble with him, Friend Owen, before this drive is finished."

Tolliver glanced at the bench rancher, then away. It seemed very strange to be having trouble with his own crew, to be depending more and more on a man he had always considered a petty outlaw. He thought, either I've misjudged Ray all these years, or he is playing some game of his own and I can't think what game it could be. He forgot it in his effort to get some sleep, but Shorty broke his sleep by saying,

"Bryan Hall sent a man ahead of us today, warning DeChute not to sell us hay."

Owen turned over to look at the tall rider. "Who told you?"

"Mrs. DeChute. She wanted to know why Bryan hated you."

Tolliver said, "Forget it," and reclosed his eyes. But although he tried, he did not sleep at once. His mind was filled with Bryan Hall, with the knowledge that the banker would not be content until he had driven Tolliver from the valley.

They made only seven miles, camping the second night at Cloud's Crossing, where the trail dipped down to ford the small river.

There was not much shelter, but the high banks and the clumps of aspen along the frozen stream gave a little protection. It was not a bad camp, as camps go, but as the night progressed the wind rose to almost a gale, and the cold grew so intense that they shivered under the shelter of the tarp which had been rigged against the sled side to form a kind of tent.

The storm increased and at daylight Owen put his horse up the short northern grade, coming into the full force of the gale and realized that it would be impossible to drive the cattle into the teeth of the wind. They stayed in camp that day, cramped and uncomfortable, not talking much, brooding over their own thoughts.

Porine was more surly than the rest, and Tolliver wisely left him entirely alone. In the early darkness they got their evening meal, the food turning cold on the tin plates before it could be spooned into their mouths.

The snow stopped at two o'clock, and the wind died until it was a murmur which hardly stirred the bare branches of the aspens. They routed the herd out at four, the animals so snow-covered that it was hard to see them in the early light. The snow was crusted, nearly a quarter of an inch thick. Not heavy enough to bear a man's weight, but hard and sharp, cutting the animal's hocks as they plowed through it.

They moved under a leaden sky, through a world that was unbroken white, the crust slowing their already slow progress, and reached Hemstead's ranch at about three.

Tolliver wanted no repeat of the friction at DeChute's and rode ahead, coming into the ranch yard without even attracting the attention of the dogs. Then someone saw him from the window and Hemstead came through the door, a worried man, long and thin with so little chin that his mouth seemed to cut across the column of his rising neck.

Owen saw by the man's eyes that he knew what they wanted and was trying hastily to frame a refusal. "I'm short of hay," he said, before Tolliver could ask him. "I hurt my back the first of August, and I didn't put up as much as usual."

Tolliver did not waste time in argument. He merely stared at the rancher, watching Hemstead's face get red with resentment and anger.

"Damnit, Owen, don't look at a man as if he is a thief because he happens to be short of hay."

"I'm not," said Tolliver. "This is my wondering expression, Dave. I'm wondering if you are speaking with your own words or those of Bryan Hall."

The man before him turned desperate. "Honest, Owen, this has nothing to do with the rider Bryan sent. It's just that I haven't enough to feed my own stock if this weather holds. You wouldn't want all my cows to die before this damn snow stops falling?"

Tolliver had seen the stacks behind the barn as he rode into the yard and he knew that Hemstead ran less than a hundred head. He said, softly, "I wouldn't want anything like that to happen of course, but I know how many you feed, and I can count your stacks."

"But they're not all mine." Hemstead sounded near tears. "The big one belongs to Honos Walters. I told you that I hurt my back and couldn't get in the hay. Honos and I made a deal. He sent his crew down to help me, taking part of the hay as payment. He simply hasn't gotten around to hauling it yet."

A glint of grim humor showed in Tolliver's eyes. "We'll use Honos' then. He shouldn't care since I'll pay the full market price and save him the trouble of hauling it besides. And Honos is one man who enjoys having others do the work for him."

Hemstead knew when he was licked. He was not a forceful character and he had always been a little afraid of Owen Tolliver.

"Honos will skin me," he said without conviction.

Tolliver's cold stiffened lips came into a real smile. "You might look well that way, your hide nailed up and salted on the barn door to dry. Can our cook use your kitchen, or would you rather we ate from the sled?"

Hemstead said pleadingly, "Honest, Owen, I'm trying not to take sides against you. I'll tell the woman. She will cook for you, but we're a little short of grub."

"Plenty in the sled." Owen pulled his horse around and headed back to the slowly on-coming herd.

CHAPTER 14

ONOS WALTERS was a different breed. A Texan with big spreading mustaches and a bull-like voice, he had been a fighter and he was a fighter still, and there was no love lost between him and the rest of the outfits in the valley.

After the Box M and Pete Daily he was the biggest owner, and he bossed the northern ranchers whether they liked it or not.

This was the last ranch where Tolliver could hope to find hay in any quantity, but he knew before he entered the big yard that Walters might be hard to handle.

Honos was explosive and slightly unpredictable and he stood beside the barn looking bulkier than usual in his heavy coat as Tolliver followed the long lane in from the distant road, squinting directly into the western sun.

Walters made no sign of greeting as Tolliver approached, nor did he ask him to step down. He stood glaring up at the man in the saddle like an angry bull who does not know quite how to begin his charge.

"You'll get no hay here, Owen. Those cows aren't going to eat Circle W feed. Keep to the road."

Owen eased himself in the saddle, saying evenly, "They've already filled their bellies on Circle W feed, Honos."

The big man stared at him suspiciously. "What are you talking about?"

"That stack of hay you had at Hemstead's. What the critters didn't eat they trampled in the snow. I figured it about four tons." He drew the glove from his right hand and dipped it into his pocket, bringing up a stack of gold pieces. "What do you say hay is worth up here?"

Walters' eyes were on the bare hand. It was known all over the valley that the man had an inherent love for gold which was transcended only by his love of violence. He swore hoarsely. "I didn't want to sell."

Tolliver held his temper. "A lot of us do things we don't want to do, Honos. I'll pay for the hay, a fair price, but only if you will sell me enough more to feed my stock for a couple of days while we lay over to rest them."

Walters seemed to swell until it looked as if he might explode. "Are you telling me that you won't pay for the hay you've already stolen unless I sell you some more?"

"That," said Tolliver, "is the general idea." He heard noise behind him and turning saw Porine and Ray Cantwine riding rapidly up the lane and frowned, wishing they had kept out of this, that they had stayed with the herd.

Walters saw them too. Walters' heavy lips pulled back from his yellow teeth in a half sneer. "It's fine company you keep, Owen. I don't want those thieving Cantwines on my land."

Tolliver did not answer.

"You hear me." Walters was suddenly furious. "You come riding in here like God Almighty and you tell me you've stolen my hay and that you'll only pay for it if I let you have some more, and on top of that you bring the Cantwines, and that rider with him is no better than they are."

Porine had brought his horse to a sliding stop. Before Owen realized what he intended he swung to the ground and with a muttered oath charged Walters. He was smaller than the big rancher, but he was quicker, and he drove a mittened hand to Walters' jaw twice before Walters managed to send over a looping hay-maker which caught the side of Porine's head and sent him flailing into the snow.

He struggled up to his knees then, tearing at the buttons which held his coat. Had not the coat been fastened Owen would not have reached him before Porine killed the rancher. But the coat was fastened and he had only two buttons open by the time Owen dropped from his horse and jumped forward.

Porine tore the last button loose and jerked at his gun, just as Owen grabbed his wrist and wrenched it free. For an instant they stared at each other and there was murder in Porine's eyes. Then Owen flipped the captured gun to Ray Cantwine, and heard Walters roar and turned, just as the bigger man jumped forward to aim a kick at Porine's side.

"Stop it." Tolliver used his shoulder to knock Walters back. "Stop it."

But Walters was past calculated thought. He was like an angry bull, tormented by picadors. He put his head down and charged Tolliver, wrapping his powerful arms about Owen's more slender body and trying to break him backwards to the ground.

Owen set his feet. He heaved outward suddenly with his own arms, breaking the man's grip and pushing him away, ducking a jabbing blow which Walters sent overhand toward his head, and stepping in close to drive a right and then a left to the heavy jaw.

Walters' head jerked back. He shook it for a moment and then charged again, swinging with both big fists. Tolliver stepped inside. He drove a short left into the stomach and then hit the man with a right just over the heart. The blow might have put Walters down had he not been wearing a heavy coat. As it was he came on in, grasping Tolliver again in his bear-like hug and carrying him from his feet.

They rolled over and over in the snow, choking,

gasping for breath, and somehow Tolliver broke free and came up to his feet and set himself, and caught Walters as the big man rose, a blow to the mouth, a second to the nose and then a clean right to the chin. Walters went over onto his back and lay there. His two men came running from the house and Cantwine stopped them with Porine's gun which he still held. They stood there, undecided, watching their boss drag himself heavily to his feet. His nose was mashed and there was a trickle of blood from a cut at the corner of his mouth.

Tolliver said, "Had enough?"

The man breathed deeply, trying to steady himself. "I guess so."

"How much is hay?"

Walters stared at him through one eye which was already puffing. "A hundred and fifty with what you've already stolen."

Porine said in sharp, angry disgust, "Gimme my gun, Cantwine, or use it on the hog yourself."

"No," said Tolliver. "We've got six men, Honos. We could take what we want, but I'll pay. Just remember. Don't ever ask me for a favor."

"I never have," Walters' voice was a grumble. He watched avidly as Tolliver counted out the gold, then pocketed it, saying harshly, "Make sure none of my cattle mix with yours."

"What about eating in your cookshack?"

"We're short of grub."

"We've got enough food. We want some place to

cook it out of the weather."

Walters pursed his bruised lips. "A dollar a man a meal."

This was more than Porine could take. He jumped toward the heavier man but Owen tripped him neatly, sending him headlong into the snow. He scrambled up, blowing furiously. "Owen, I'll not forget that. First you take a man's gun, then you send him down. You don't want loyalty."

"I don't want a fight," Owen said. "Not now, not until the cattle are delivered."

He knew from the look in the man's eyes that Porine would not forget, that his attitude would never be quite the same again. But he ignored Porine, saying to Walters, "You're a thief and a swindler, but I'll pay because we haven't the time to fight." He turned then and lifted himself wearily onto his horse, and rode back to help with the herd. Behind him Cantwine was arguing with Porine and he heard Porine say,

"He called you names too, Ray."

And Cantwine's answer. "Names don't mean anything, my friend. There will be the chance to settle with Walters later, after this is finished, if I still want to then." He laughed and Tolliver could not understand the laugh. He only knew that his men were following, that trouble had been averted for the moment.

The following day was bright, and clear and warm, the thermometer on the Circle W bunkhouse reading forty-six. They rested, having the place much to themselves for Walters and his men had withdrawn to the big house.

Porine was sullen, hardly answering when he was spoken to and Owen would not have been surprised to see the man mount his horse and head back for town.

But Porine was still with them when they drove the cattle out toward the road the following morning. The sky was no longer clear and the sun came up to cast its rays weakly through a mat of clouds. It was cold again, and the wind whipped at the crusted snow, swirling what it could pry loose in little eddies which beat against their faces with the stinging force of shot.

They made only six miles before they pulled into a hayless camp in the shelter of a rock butte. The cattle had not liked the facing wind, and a good third of the animals were nursing snow-cut legs.

The horses were nearly as bad and the men found themselves shifting mounts at two hour periods. Also they lost their first stock that day, five animals which would no longer keep up and which were abandoned beside the trail on the off chance that they might drift before the wind back to Walters.

The camp was a dismal one. Mac had developed a hacking cough and Porine still nursed his grievance in sullen silence. Tolliver ignored him, helping the old cook whose feet had taken on a touch of chilblains and who was limping badly.

They all had colds, but Mac was the worst and Tolliver relieved him from his stint of night riding, ordering him to stay as warm as possible in his blankets. The wind increased, the cattle shifted uneasily.

None of them slept much and at breakfast Porine and Cantwine almost came to blows over a cup of coffee.

Tolliver separated them wearily, and they lifted themselves into the saddle in sultry silence, the soggy breakfast lying in an undigestible lump at the pits of their stomachs.

It was not snowing, but the wind was still a driving force into which the cattle headed with studied reluctance and it took them the full day to make the five short miles to the Pattons' sorry place.

The Patton brothers were shiftless and sullen, running only a few cows, spending most of the summer months fitfully mining in the hills which ran down from the western mountains to a few hundred yards behind their house.

This place had once belonged to Bryan Hall's father and Tolliver could not help comparing Hall's present stature with his simple beginnings. The banker had come a long way and in all fairness it had to be admitted that he had had little help, but had achieved his success purely by his own effort.

In another man Tolliver would have found the progress admirable, but he could not in his heart admire Hall or anything that the man did. Their rivalry ran back a long way, and it had never been a friendly one, although they had escaped an open break until this trouble began. But he realized that it was too deep a feeling ever to be healed. As long as both he and Hall remained in the valley there would be some kind of warfare between them.

He came into the yard to learn that the Pattons had no hay, but there was wood and warmth in their two room cabin which they shared without protest.

"Help yourself," Ken Patton said. "We're pulling out tomorrow. Too much snow and no feed. We'll drive the stock down to Walters and go on to town. May go on to Cap Rock and maybe get a winter job with the railroad."

"How about riding up with us? I'll pay fifty and found."

They considered the suggestion, their eyes neutral, and rejected it. "You won't get through," Ken Patton told him. "I talked with the Indian boy that brought you the word. The Devil's Cut is nearly full. Did he tell you that?"

Tolliver shook his head. "I'm not worrying about the Cut," he said. "The Indians will meet us at the pass. We should have a hundred braves to help. With that many we can almost carry them on our backs."

"Then you don't need us." It was obvious that the brothers wanted no part of the drive. They had had enough snow already to last them for one winter.

Porine spoke from beyond the stove. "Maybe we'd be smart to listen to them. They know this part of the country better than we do."

Owen looked at him. The change in Porine since the fight at Walters was noticeable indeed. The fire had all gone out of the man, and along with it his desire to keep riding for the Box M. It was, Tolliver sensed, only a matter of time now until Porine would drift. He shrugged away the thought, changing the subject by asking, "Will we find any hay at Brady's?"

"Some hay," Ken Patton said. "Not much, but take what you find because there is no one there. Brady went out in October. He hurt his foot and headed back for Indiana. It's not my place to tell you what to do, Owen, but if it was me I'd leave the cattle at Brady's and ride ahead and bring down the Indians. Once you get into the pass there won't be too much chance of turning around. From Brady's you might make it back to Honos' if the worst came to the worst."

Porine said, "What could be worse than what we've had?"

Ken Patton looked at him and shrugged. "You get a three day ice storm in the hills and you'll know what I'm talking about. Then you'd realize that you have seen nothing yet."

Mac coughed and looking at him Tolliver saw the fever patches on the man's cheeks and frowned. "If you aren't better by morning, Mac, you go out with the Pattons."

The rider stared at him with dull eyes. "I'll be all right." But he said it without conviction, like a man who was only trying to reassure himself.

Tolliver knew that every man in the room was looking at him, and judging him and he tried to judge himself, to put aside all stubbornness and weigh the chances of ultimate success. They had come this far. It was eleven miles to Brady's and then less than five miles to the mouth of the pass. From the mouth, up through the twisting hills it was only twenty-four miles to the Indian agent's house.

His mouth hardened. They had come this far and they would go on. It did not matter what the Pattons did, or Porine. They would go on. And then he turned and glanced at the Cantwines and wondered anew why they were still with him and how long they would stay and put his question into words, saying, "What do you think, Ray?"

Ray Cantwine shrugged, and took time to light a splinter through the ventilator of the stove door and fire his pipe. "We aren't in too bad shape," he said, "outside of the animals that are limping. I don't know how much snow there is in the pass, but if it were me I'd shove ahead to see."

Porine was staring at him. "I don't get it," he said. "You couldn't be pushing harder if all those Indians were your relatives, or if all the cattle were yours and the money they'll bring was already in your pocket."

Cantwine laughed. "Don't put wishful ideas into my head, Porine."

Porine grunted, rose and stomped out of the cabin. Cantwine's eyes found Tolliver's and they held for a moment, then the bench rancher looked away saying in an even voice, "Morning comes early. I'm for the blankets."

Mac was even worse in the morning, and they left him for the Patton brothers to load upon their sled, and pushed out. The day was neither good nor bad. The wind was down, but it was thoroughly cold, and the clouds threatened although the snow held off.

They lost ten more steers and two horses, too badly leg-cut to continue. One of the beeves they shot and butchered out, loading the choicer pieces upon the sled and forging on, driving until a good hour after the early darkness had settled before they turned the limping animals into the yard of the abandoned ranch.

Brady's was a picture of neglect. The door of the house had not been fastened properly. The wind had opened it and the single room was drifted half full of snow.

They shoveled it out. They built a roaring fire in the rusted stove, and after they had bedded the cattle and thrown down the single small stack of hay they ate huge steaks, huddled about the cherry red stove.

The log walls were badly chinked, and the cloth liner was torn so that the wind sucked in. It was very cold outside. Porine sulked in the corner and some of his ill temper was being transferred to the rest of the crew.

Even Shorty had quarrelled with the cook about the evening coffee, and by morning the feeling in the small cabin was no better. Tolliver sensed that the crew was falling apart, that the high spirit of adventure with which they had begun this drive was gone.

He hurried them through breakfast purposely. It was better that they have something to occupy their minds. They pushed the cattle out onto the trail and started upward toward the mouth of the pass four miles away.

To Tolliver it seemed that they were starting on the last lap, that their troubles should be nearly ended.

Tonight or tomorrow night they should make contact with the Indians. From then on they would have probably more help than they needed.

CHAPTER 15

THEY CAMPED IN TIMBER the next night, four miles up the canyon from the mouth of the pass. They had begun to climb almost as soon as they left the Brady yard, following the winding stream, coming first to thick stands of aspen which gradually gave way to piñon.

It was gruelling work and the progress slowed until it seemed to Tolliver that the herd barely moved. It took two hours to cover a mile, three hours to cover the next, but when they finally had their camp established it was reasonably warm.

After the wood was cut, the cook fire flaming, they laboriously cleared enough of the stream ice to haze the stock down for an evening drink. When this was done and supper eaten Tolliver dug out a box of cigars which he had hidden in the cook sled and passed them around.

Those who were not riding with the cattle stretched out under the shelter of the tarp, easing their cramped and tightened muscles.

In the firelight they were a villainous looking crew. Frost and wind had burned their cheeks until each man could boast raw patches where the skin had actually been weathered away. None had shaved, and their washing had been sketchy to say the least.

There was a certain air of relaxation about the camp, as if they all felt that the ordeal was nearly finished. Even Porine was a little more relaxed, and Ray Cantwine was smiling broadly.

Tolliver put their thoughts into words. "Once we make contact with the Indians we'll let them worry about getting the cattle through. An Indian is lazy until he gets hungry; then they'll work like hell."

They rolled in, but they did not get much sleep for the wind came up, and by morning a full gale was raging down the canyon's throat.

In one way the wind actually helped, for on the long straight stretches between the curves it literally lifted the snow from the ground, banking it in tremendous drifts against the outcroppings on the inside of the turns, but leaving the center of their path almost bare.

They forced their way upward against the freezing blast, chilled and mean and nearly wordless from the constant buffeting of the flying snow.

But at nightfall they came into a small meadow where the canyon walls widened into a kind of bowl. Above them was a sharp curve which offered a degree of protection and they pulled the sled close under the overhanging wall and built a huge fire which warmed them as they ate a belated supper beneath the shelter of the tent-like tarp.

Tolliver rode around the bedded herd, looking them over with critical eye. It was amazing how much weight the animals had lost. The tallow was entirely gone and they were thinned down until their skins hung loose and the bones showed so sharply that it seemed they must burst through the covering.

It snowed during the night, not too heavily but the wind was still strong, swirling it through the driving air until the night riders were blanketed by the stuff.

Tolliver came in finally, pausing to drink a scalding cup of coffee from the blackened pot, and found Porine awake, huddled by the fire, his returning good humor gone.

He said, savagely, "You'd think those Indians would come down here to find us instead of waiting at the head of the pass. That's the trouble with trying to help people, the more help you give them the more they expect."

Cantwine stirred and rolled over. "Why don't you shut up and get some sleep?"

Porine said, "Make me."

They glared at each other in the dancing fire light. The whole camp was awake by now. The old cook rose, grumbling, and moved out toward the fire, warming his hands before he started to get breakfast.

"It's the wind," Porine said. "I always hated wind, ever since I was a kid. We can't drive against it, Owen."

Tolliver agreed.

"Why in hell don't those blasted Indians come down after their beef? They should certainly smell our smoke, or see it."

"The wind's coming down the canyon." Tolliver rose

to help the cook. He worked methodically, his mind a little numb from tiredness and from loss of sleep, and from the cold.

They ate, and afterward he rose, knowing that every man around the fire was looking at him, awaiting his decision.

"We'll hold them here," he said. "From what I remember of the upper canyon there isn't another bedground between here and the Devil's Cut. I'll ride ahead until I find those Indians."

He turned without waiting for their answer and moving out to the rough holding corral they had set up against the bank, he saddled a fresh horse.

The animal was limping as he headed it up the steepening trail. All the horses were limping, but they had not lost the flesh the cattle had. A horse could pick up feed where a cow could not. A horse would paw down through banked snow for bunch grass below.

He came around the sheltering curve onto a straight upward climb and the howling wind nearly carried him out of the saddle. He bent his head against it, riding on, noting that the trail ahead was swept almost clear of snow. If the wind would only do the same for the Devil's Cut, but he knew that it was a forlorn hope. The Cut was a twisting defile, carved through the harder rim-rock by the tireless stream. At places it was hardly more than twenty feed wide, its sheer walls rising a good thousand feet above the tortuous trail below. It would, he was certain, be badly drifted, how badly he had no way of judging until he reached it.

Each bend that he rounded brought him nearer to the Cut and therefore nearer to where the Indian camp should be, but he reached a point only a mile below the Cut and still there was no smell of smoke on the wind, no sign of smoke in the sky.

He looked ahead with a feeling of growing helplessness. It seemed impossible that the Indians would not have come, that they would not be waiting for the arrival of the cattle. And if they weren't here he had no idea that his exhausted crew could proceed without them. If the Indians weren't here he had failed. The herd would perish in the pass unless they could turn them around and somehow work their way back to Walters' ranch.

His mind was so occupied that he did not realize how thoroughly chilled he was. He rode on, his eyes searching the cleft of the sky ahead, looking for a trace of smoke, for sign of the camp which must be somewhere in the snowy hills above him.

But there was no sign. He came around the last twisting turn and saw the canyon sides pinch ahead and knew that he was looking upwards at the mouth of the Cut, and felt his heart sink for there was no sign of anyone. He was utterly alone in a frosted world.

As he climbed upward he knew that the worst of his fears were fully realized. Snow had drifted in the Cut, piling until it made a barrier nearly a hundred feet deep, as impassable as if it were a granite wall.

He checked his horse, feeling his anger surge up at the elements that had conspired to defeat him, at the

Indian agent for failing to buy his beef at the proper time, at Johnny Short Bear and the other Indians for not being here as promised.

Even with the huge drift they might get the meat through if there was enough help. It was impossible to climb from the lower side, but coming down from the reservation on snowshoes the tribesmen should have been able to break through. With them here the herd could be moved, even if it were necessary to butcher the animals in the pass and pack the meat upward on their backs.

But the Indians weren't here. There was nothing here save the howling wind and swirling snow. He was alone, as alone as he had ever been in his life.

They had come so close, so very close. It was only four miles from the upper end of the Cut to the reservation buildings, five miles in all, yet to all practical purposes it might have been a thousand.

He sat staring at the mountain of white which rose between the rock walls like a dam to block the runoff of a canyon, and slowly pulled his horse around, defeated, ready to attempt to drive the herd out, to salvage what animals he could.

And then he saw the end of the snowshoe sticking out of the edge of a drift on the right of the trail and halted his horse.

He sat staring down at it for a moment. Only the front part of the webbing showed, the rest was buried by the soft whiteness.

He stepped down stiffly, looping the rein over his

arm to keep the tired horse from drifting and stood another minute, looking down at the silent marker, knowing what he would find and yet hesitating to investigate.

Afterward he fastened the horse to a stunted pine and began to dig. He dug with his gloved hands since he had no tools to use. The snow was crusted, but below the top was soft and not tightly packed.

Still, it took nearly an hour to extricate Johnny Short Bear's frozen body. He knew now why the Indians were not camped in the pass. The word that he was coming with the herd had never reached the reservation.

Johnny Short Bear had not gotten home. As soon as he had freed the body from its icy resting place the whole story was as plain to read as if the Indian boy had left a written message.

The left leg was doubled crookedly, the splintered bone thrusting out through the frozen flesh. It was obvious that the boy had attempted to scale the canyon wall to the ridge above, to bypass the huge drift which blocked the Cut ahead.

Somewhere up the slippery rock face he had lost his footing and tumbled back down the precipitous slope. His leg shattered, he had tried to drag himself back onto the trail and had not quite made it, or perhaps he had been knocked unconscious by the fall and had frozen to death, the drifting snow covering his small body as if an ashamed nature were trying to make amends.

Owen Tolliver squatted beside the dead boy for a long moment. A little while before he had been angry at the Indians for not being in the pass. He had been ready to turn the herd back and try and save what cows he could.

But his anger was gone. The boy had given his life in an effort to help his tribe and they were even now probably waiting in their lodges, wondering if Joe John and the valley people had forsaken them.

He bent forward and with difficulty loosened the ice-covered thongs which had held the snowshoes to Johnny's feet and straightening fastened them behind his saddle. Then he mounted and rode slowly back down the canyon toward the waiting crew.

He knew before he reached camp that there would be protests. He had kept the crew moving with the hope that within a few miles the Indians would relieve them of the herd. Now the Indians weren't coming, and the Cut was blocked, the storm at his back increasing.

He wasted no pity on the dead boy, no sentiment for his untimely passing. His full worry was directed in an effort to help those who were still living. The dead had nothing to worry about. It was the people on the reservation above who were out of food. Somehow they had to get the word that the herd was in the canyon, that there was plenty of beef if they would only come and get it. They had to get the word. He had to take it to them because there was no other way. He stared at the snowing ridges above him, wondering if he could get through.

CHAPTER 16

PORINE SAID, "That's the end of it." He had risen from his spot beside the fire as Tolliver came down the canyon, and he had listened as Owen told them about finding the Indian's body, his face turning angry as he heard that there was no help at the end of the pass.

"Well, let's get out of here."

Tolliver looked at the others. The old cook was huddled before the fire, wrapped in a blanket. Shorty was shivering. Only the Cantwines and the Mex seemed unaffected by the news. It was as if they had reached a point where nothing mattered.

"We'd better butcher a steer," Porine said, "and take the sled and see if we can get down. We'll be lucky if we reach Brady's. There isn't a sound horse in the whole bunch."

Tolliver said, "I don't blame you."

Porine stared at him. "Meaning what?" His tone was truculent, as if he felt an inner need to take his spite out on someone, on anyone.

"Meaning what I said." Tolliver got down stiffly and moved in to the heat of the fire. "You've all taken more than any men should be asked to take. Get your horses and ride out. I think the cattle will stay in the meadow. They will at least until this wind dies."

Porine snorted. "Sounds like you're not going with us. What are you going to do?"

"Take that Indian's snowshoes and try to climb over the ridge. He tried to get up the canyon wall at the mouth of the Cut. It's too steep there, but I can reach the top from here, and follow that hogback over." He pointed above their heads.

"Now I know you're crazy." Porine turned to the others as if for aid. "We can't let him do it. He's in no shape to start. Even if he were rested it would be a long chance."

Tolliver ignored him. He moved over to the sled and without disturbing the cook began to make up a package of dried beef, a loaf of bread and a sack of coffee. To this he added one of the smaller kettles and wrapped the whole into a light pack.

They watched him with sunken eyes. Porine swore hoarsely. "I never ran out on a man in my life, but that doesn't hold for fools. I'm going back down the trail."

Tolliver turned. "You don't have to make excuses," he said. "You've all done more than I expected. Get your sled loaded, and kill a beef."

"I ain't going." It was the old cook. "I'll stay here until Owen gets back."

Tolliver looked at him, the harsh lines of his face softening. "No. Porine's right."

"I'll stay." The cook was stubborn with the crankiness of age. "I never yet started any place that I turned back, and I'm too old to change."

Tolliver knew the man. He merely shrugged and turned his head. "Shorty, will you stay with the cook?"

The tall man nodded silently. Tolliver had not even

151

looked at the Cantwines. He assumed that they would pull out with Porine. He was in fact surprised that they had come this far. He said to them now in his tired voice, "I won't try to thank you boys. If I can help you later, say the word."

Ray Cantwine grinned. "We'll stick."

Tolliver looked at him, still not comprehending, and Ray said, "There's twenty cows in that herd that I claim. I'll stay around until they're delivered. So will Charley."

"I go." It was the Mexican. "She get too cold up top I think." It was almost the first sentence he had uttered since the drive began.

Tolliver nodded. He reached into his pocket and pulled out two twenty dollar gold pieces and put them into the man's dirty hand.

"You've got a place at the Box M any time." He looked back at Cantwine. "You wait here three days. If you haven't heard from me by that time, take the cook and Shorty and pull out."

"I'll hear from you," Cantwine told him as Tolliver stooped and fastened on the snowshoes he had taken from Johnny Short Bear. "You'll get through. I've watched you for several years, Owen. I never saw you stopped yet."

It was praise that Tolliver had not expected, and he flushed in embarrassment as he straightened and retied the handkerchief which bound his hat down and adjusted the second one across his mouth.

Porine was still sullen and angry, and Owen went to

him and placed a hand on his shoulder. "It's all right," he said. "You and the Mex go on back to the ranch and take care of things until I come. We don't know what's happening there."

Porine did not meet his eyes, and he knew without being told that Porine would not be at the ranch when he returned. The man was through with the Box M, through with the valley. The chances were that they would not meet again.

The thought saddened Owen. He had neither liked nor disliked the Irishman, but Porine had been a good hand and he had certainly carried more than his share during this drive. He debated paying him off at once and decided against it, feeling that Porine would rather sacrifice the portion of his pay he had coming than have it recognized by all that he was quitting now.

But Tolliver forgot Porine as soon as he began to climb. The slope was slippery and steep, and the snow had banked up between the trees into drifts which, had he sunk into them, would have been well above his head.

The snow was crusted, but not enough to support his weight without the webs, and although the temperature was nearly zero, the exertion of the climb had him sweating beneath his heavy clothes.

Twice he slipped and fell, but each time his sliding body was checked by one of the twisted pines which clung to the sharp face of the canyon wall, and he topped out finally, reaching the hogback which separated the pass from the smaller canyon to the west.

Here he paused to get his breath, peering downward through the trees toward the camp a thousand feet below him. The timber in between was thick enough that he would not have known its exact location save for the smoke curling up from the fire.

The smoke gave him an idea and he turned into the pines, breaking off half a dozen dead branches. The snow here was a good ten feet deep and he found himself able to reach halfway up the gnarled trunks. He built his small fire away from the snow covered trees, and threw snow into the kettle and added a short handful of coffee, and while he waited for it to boil, chewed doggedly upon some of the dried meat strips.

Now that he was no longer moving the sweat within his clothes gave them a clammy feel and he shivered, crouching behind a tree trunk to escape the full sweep of the wind.

Afterward he started along the peak of the ridge, moving with care. At times it was a thousand feet wide, at others so narrow that a slip in either direction would send him hurtling into one or other of the canyons.

He came to a break in the hogback and it took him an hour to work his way around it. By this time the sun had dropped from sight in the west and a cloud bank was building up in the north.

He kept going as the night shut down. Weariness swept over him in waves, and his feet felt made of lead, so that each step was a separate effort.

Below him, somewhere to his right, was the snow filled Devil's Cut, ahead of him a heavy stand of timber. He came into the trees, thankful for their shelter, yet not daring to pause, knowing that if he ceased to move he would be more than apt to go to sleep. He wanted sleep, but its invitation now was an invitation to death.

He chewed on the dried meat until his jaws ached. He beat his gloved hands together. His legs below the knees had lost all sensation, and yet he moved forward, slowly, very slowly now, feeling each tree trunk to tell him which way was north.

His great fear was of circling in the darkness. He moved on, and as the sky lightened in the east he came down slowly off the ridge to the irregular plateau beyond, and when the sun climbed he saw the reservation buildings in the distance.

He went forward, more surely now, one foot, then the other. He began to repeat it to himself aloud, left, now right, left, now right. The sun increased, the glare from the snow around him was almost unbearable upon his eyes. He would have halted to make himself some coffee, but he had now left the timber well behind. All around him was snow, and more snow, and still more snow, glittering, blinding him.

He held his eyes almost closed and he kept going, his feet dragging, left, now right, left, now right. Twice he realized that he was standing perfectly still, thinking that his feet were moving, and was frightened to realize that he had no idea how long he had been motionless.

Once he fell, and he had great difficulty in getting to

his feet again. The snow did not seem quite as deep here, but it was over three feet. He had to unfasten the snowshoes to rise, and his chilled fingers made the task almost impossible.

Afterward, he figured that it took him six hours to make the four miles from the end of the pass to the reservation buildings, but at the time he neither knew nor cared. The buildings were closer now. He could see the smoke rising from the chimneys into the clear air, and then he could see the winter quarters of the Indians, pitched close to the agent's house, to the reservation store.

He felt that someone must see him, that someone would come out to meet him, but no one came, and he could not go on. He knew that he could not go on. If he could only lie down and sleep, sleep for a little while.

Drowsiness rode up in waves. He wasn't moving. He was again standing still, looking at the distant buildings. But he must be moving because they seemed closer, they were closer, and then he was suddenly among the Indian quarters, and the snow here had been trampled into paths, and people stared at him from the lodge doorways, and then he fell.

He remembered later the babble of their excited voices, and the thought that those who said Indians never showed emotion were entirely wrong. And then he knew that he was being helped to his feet and that a dozen hands had lifted him, and he was being carried to the big log house which was the Indian agent's residence.

CHAPTER 17

EDWARD LORD was crying. Edward Lord was a religious and well meaning man for all his lack of ability and judgment. He was small, and his face was thin and his nose pointed. His wife was large, and she had a certain competence which her husband lacked.

She worked the wet boots from Tolliver's feet and packed snow around them and she kept telling him that everything would be all right, that she had seen worse cases of frostbite back in Indiana.

And Lord with tears streaming down his face told Tolliver that he had prayed and that Tolliver's effort was an answer to his prayers, that there was only food on the reservation for less than one week, that Lord meant to write to the Indian Bureau as soon as the trails were open and describe to them what a great humanitarian thing it was which Tolliver had done.

Owen had to listen to him. There was no escaping the small man's sharp, nasal voice. He wished only that Lord would go away and let him sleep. He felt that if he did not sleep at once he would go stark mad. He wanted to scream at the man, but lacked the strength.

He did say finally that Lord was counting things before they were finished, that the cattle weren't at the reservation, but in the pass, below the snow filled Devil's Cut.

The Indian agent blinked at him. "I've sent for the

Chief," he said. "The Chief will take his people and they will bring back the cattle."

The Chief came. Owen Tolliver had no idea how old the man was. He had been older than Joe John, but there was no telling how much older.

He came into the room, still straight, still walking solidly and proudly. He came over to the rocker in which Tolliver sat and said in his quiet voice,

"You do Joe John proud. I knew he would send someone."

Tolliver remembered then that Johnny Short Bear had not come home and that these people did not know that both he and Joe John were dead. He did not try to tell them. He saved his strength for what he felt must be said.

"There's ten to thirty feet of snow in the Cut," he told the Indian. "The cattle are in a meadow three miles below there. You'll either have to break a trail through, packing the snow so it will hold the cattle, or butcher them down there and carry them up on your backs."

He didn't hear what the Indian answered. It was as if he had held himself awake merely to say that much. He leaned back in the rocker and despite the burning needles in his feet, he went to sleep. Somehow Lord and his wife got him across the room and into bed. They tried to wake him for food four hours later, but they did not succeed. He slept, and as Cantwine said, he was one of the few men in the world who completed a cattle drive lying flat on his back.

Cantwine was telling him about it the next afternoon.

Cantwine said, "You know how I feel about Indians. The world would be a lot better off if they had never been around, but I have to give those warwhoops credit. They came waltzing down there near three hundred strong, men and squaws. The first thing they did was to butcher twenty head, and you should have seen them light into that beef. You'd have thought they hadn't had a thing to eat this year. They'd come down through the Cut, most of them on snowshoes, and they sure packed it down, but after they finished eating I figured they'd lost their minds. They start gathering wood, and the next thing we know they've got a string of fires built clear the length of the Cut. I was sure they were crazy then. I thought they were trying to melt all that snow out of there, and I knew that wouldn't work. There isn't enough wood in the world for that."

Tolliver was again sitting in the rocking chair, fully dressed except for his boots, for his feet were so swollen and tender that he could not get into them.

"Well, what did they do?"

"They did what they planned. They burned those fires half the night, then they let them go out. The snow the heat melted ran down into the stuff below and froze solid. They built a bridge of ice across the whole mile of that snow pack, solid enough that a cow's hoof wouldn't sink into it. We left the cook sled at the meadow and rode up here. We came through first; The Indians are bringing the cows up now."

Tolliver stared at him. "Still a job, getting those brutes up over that ice."

"With three hundred hungry Indians working at it, you could do anything." Cantwine grinned and extended his feet toward the stove. "This is comfort. Only trouble is, it's a reservation and the agent has no whiskey."

Tolliver shrugged and closed his eyes. He was yet too tired to care.

"You're a hero." Ray Cantwine's tone had taken on its old note of mockery. "I told them Joe John and the boy were dead, and that if it hadn't been for you they'd never have seen one single steer. I wouldn't be surprised if they made you a chief. It might be an idea. Some ways it isn't too bad to be a warwhoop, with fool white men breaking their necks to drive beef up to you."

Tolliver did not answer. Cantwine stretched and rose and walked over to the window, peering out. "Those redskins better hustle that beef along. It looks like it's going to snow again, and plenty. Me, I'm getting a little fed up with snow. I was in Laredo, Texas, when I was a kid and I liked it there and I wonder why I ever came into this forsaken country."

It was the most Cantwine had ever said about his life before coming to the valley, and Owen Tolliver opened his eyes and regarded him.

"Ray," he said, "before this drive started you were the last man in the world I'd have picked for the job. Why does a man like you choose to live the way you do?"

For an instant there was a hot, intemperate look in

Cantwine's eyes, then he masked it with his usual mockery, saying, "Don't preach, Friend Owen. Don't be a reformer like Lord."

"I'm not," said Tolliver. "But you puzzle me. A person with your ability could do better than a two-bit bench outfit, having to eat his neighbors' beef to stay alive."

"I'm thinking of it," said Cantwine. "I've been thinking of it for some time." He turned then and moved over to the door, pulling it open and letting a gust of cold air in before he closed it behind him.

Tolliver stared at the closed door, then shrugged and leaning back, went to sleep. When he roused an hour later the lamps were lighted and it was snowing heavily outside. At nine Edward Lord came in, his coat white but his eyes shining.

"They've got the last of the cattle through the Cut. I've never seen the Indians work so hard, not in the two years I've been here."

Tolliver thought, hunger does strange things to people. Some it turns into savages, others it makes into willing workers. He rose and walked to the window. The snow made so solid a curtain now that it reflected the house lights.

"It's lucky they're out of the Cut, but will they make the reservation?"

"They'll make it," said the agent. There was real pride in his voice, and Tolliver thought with quickened surprise, why, he actually loves these people. It's too bad he hasn't more ability, more common sense.

Sometimes it took more than love to handle a people, it took guidance and discipline, and a sure touch of authority.

Old Joe John had had that. Old Joe John for all that he had been good to the settlers coming into the valley had also held them with a tight rein. Joe John had been a natural leader, and few had stood against him.

Tolliver thought bitterly as he watched the falling snow that he himself had failed. He had attempted to handle things as the old man would have done, and he had lacked the sure touch, the steady, driving push with which the old rancher had controlled his neighbors.

He turned back, walking over toward the kitchen door, for the agent's wife had called them to the evening meal. They ate heartily, Cantwine and his brother sitting on one side, the old cook and Tolliver on the other. From the table's end Edward Lord asked grace, thanking a gracious God for permitting the cattle to get safely through and so rectify a mistake which Lord freely admitted that he had made.

That, thought Tolliver, was the reason you could not dislike the man, even when you cursed him as a fool. He admitted his mistakes with child-like candor, and he was lavish with his praise of others. The trouble was that he learned little from experience. He would make an error again and yet again, and the lives of four hundred government wards depended on his judgment.

Cantwine had begun a teasing argument. He questioned Lord about the policy of the Indian Bureau, about its functions and its justifications.

Listening, Tolliver knew that the brush rider was baiting the man, and was tempted to interfere and did not. He thought that Cantwine necessarily must always find someone to bait, someone who was not as sharp witted as he. It was a form of strengthening his own ego, reassuring himself that he was smarter than those around him.

Apparently Ray Cantwine had spent most of his life seeking such reassurance, and yet his life for all his sharpness was one of unquestioned failure. Watching the man Tolliver realized that Cantwine knew this and that the knowledge galled him horribly, and that he wore his mask of mocking disdain to hide his true feelings from the watching world.

After the meal Cantwine and Shorty and Lord shrugged into their coats and went out to see how the Indians were making it with the cattle. Tolliver made no effort to leave the house. His feet were much too tender to attempt his boots.

He stood in the window and looked at the curtain of the snow. It was so heavy now that it blotted out the Indian village only a few hundred feet away.

It continued to snow the next day, and the next. And afterward they had an ice storm which raged for three full days, and then more snow.

No one had ever seen anything like it in the history of living man, and Edward Lord went around shaking his head and thanking Providence that they had arrived with the cattle in time.

Tolliver was getting very tired of Edward Lord and

of Cantwine, and Cantwine's brother, and of Shorty. He knew what was the matter. He was getting cabin fever.

He'd heard of it before, men snowed in together, getting on each other's nerves until they finally came to violence, and he watched himself and the others closely.

They played cards endlessly, only venturing outside the house to the enormous woodpile and the agency store. A second ice storm struck them, coating the world with a hard crust which was strong enough to bear the weight of a horse.

And then it cleared, and Edward Lord counted out the gold in payment for the steers. The stuff was heavy, nearly thirty pounds in weight.

Owen paid Cantwine for his twenty steers and divided the remainder into two equal packs, giving one to Shorty to carry. They started out on snowshoes, making no attempt to take horses with them.

The crust was solid enough here, but they might well strike spots where it would not hold a horse and where the animal would be more hindrance than help.

Slowly they worked their way toward the distant ridge. The wind was at their backs, a biting wind which swept over the frozen surface in angry gusts as if enraged that the snow was so cemented with ice that it refused to swirl.

It was very cold, and the snow beneath them as they crossed the rolling flatlands was now six feet deep.

Before noon the old cook was beginning to fag out.

He had not walked this far in fifty years, for most of his traveling had been on his chuck wagon or upon a horse.

They reached the pass and found it now nearly snowed full, and moved down the grade which was glazed and as treacherous as a toboggan slide.

The cook fell twice, the second time twisting his leg so that he could not walk. Somehow they got him to the bottom. The cold was intense, but they pushed on to the sheltered meadow where they had held the cattle, improvising a kind of sled with pine boughs on which the cook rode.

Here they built a fire, breaking limbs from the cold-brittle trees. The branches were coated with a sheath of ice nearly an inch thick, and the abandoned cook sled was buried in snow. They dug it out, for the sled held food, and after the fire was going Owen Tolliver examined the cook's leg. As nearly as he could tell there were no fractured bones, but the knee was badly swelled and so stiff that the leg would not bend. The old man was in obvious pain and Tolliver looked at Cantwine, who was watching.

Ray Cantwine said, "He needs a doctor. I saw a knee like that once, horse fell on a man, stiff the rest of his life."

Tolliver stared at the surrounding darkness. It was snowing again, spitting downward in a soft drape which seemed to close them off from the rest of the world.

"Wish we had horses for the sled. We can't drag him

clear to town by hand, but maybe we can make Brady's by tomorrow night."

They made Brady's abandoned ranch by the following evening. They took turns, in teams of two, hauling the cook on a crude toboggan which they built of boards torn from the cook sled. The were nearly exhausted before they had the fire going in the old stove of the deserted ranch house.

While Shorty and the Cantwines cooked supper Tolliver went back outside to have a last look at the weather. "I think it's clearing," he said. "Someone can push on to the Walters place in the morning, send for a doctor, borrow horses and a sled and come back here for the cook. Which would you rather do, Ray, go to Walters' or wait here?"

Ray Cantwine seemed to consider. His long narrow face beneath the sheltering curl of his three week old beard was gaunt and haggard. "Charley ain't so well," he indicated his silent brother, hunched behind the stove, spooning smoking beans slowly from his heaped plate. "We'd better wait here. I got enough grub for three or four days. You and Shorty go."

Tolliver looked at Shorty. The tall rider merely nodded. They bedded down as soon as the meal was finished. Tolliver got up four times during the night to replenish the stove and to look at the cook. It was very cold outside and the wind came through the chinks of the old walls endlessly, but by morning it had cleared.

They breakfasted before daylight. Then Tolliver took the heavy pouches of gold and laid them on the table.

He glanced up in time to catch the mocking light in Cantwine's eyes, and said easily,

"You boys can play cards while we're gone. Use these for chips, but make certain they're still here when we get back."

Cantwine was grinning. "If there wasn't any snow outside would you leave me alone with that, Friend Owen?"

Owen Tolliver grinned back. "But there is snow." He walked over to the cook, saying in a heartening tone, "With luck I'll be back here with a sled some time tomorrow. Don't try any dancing on that leg." He turned then and went out, followed by Shorty. Cantwine came into the door to watch them, and when they passed over the rise five minutes later they looked back. He was still standing motionless in the doorway.

They made the Patton place by noon, and found it deserted, and paused only to eat and went on. The wind was down, but the sky above their heads was leaden, promising more snow. It was eleven miles to Honos Walters' and they moved out, their tracks marking the only passage on the unbroken road.

Both were young, both were strong, and they walked forward steadily, but darkness was an hour old before they reached the gate and turned into the long lane which led back to the Walters' yard.

Dogs announced their arrival as they neared the house, and the door came open, throwing its beam of yellow light across the whiteness, and Walters' voice demanded to know who they were.

Tolliver called out, and they loosened their snow-shoes and stamped in, the rush of overheated air making their frosted cheeks sting.

Tolliver removed his gloves, beating his hands to restore the circulation, and turned to find Walters staring at him as if he were a ghost. He said in rising impatience, "We could use some coffee if you have some, and a horse for Shorty to push on for town, and a team and sled for me."

Walters continued to stare at him. He said slowly, dully, all his bluster gone, "I never expected to see you alive again."

Owen Tolliver glanced at Shorty, at Walters' two men and back at the Texan. "Why not?"

Walters' voice was still the dull, unaccustomed note. "Porine came through here two weeks ago. He said the herd was stalled in the pass, and that you had pushed ahead on snowshoes. And then the ice storm hit. No man or beast could have lived through that in the open."

"We weren't in the open." Tolliver moved past him toward the kitchen and found a pot of coffee on the rear of the big stove. "We were safe at the reservation."

"But you lost the cattle." Walters' shoulders rose and fell in a tired gesture.

"We got the cattle through. The Indians have them."

The man breathed deeply, as if to control himself, and his tone gained bitterness as he said, "The Box M always has been lucky, Owen. So you got through, when none of us thought you could. Did you get paid for the animals?"

"I got paid," Owen's tone was short. He had found cups and filled one for Shorty, then one for himself.

"Fool lucky. Fool lucky." Walters' tone was rising. "Five days of ice storm, on top of all the snow. Five days when a man could hardly step out of his house. We couldn't hold them. They drifted before the wind. We found some of them clear across the valley, against the east rim, frozen."

Tolliver had been lifting the cup to his lips. He lowered it suddenly. "What are you talking about?"

"Dead," said Walters. "All dead. Winter-killed. There aren't a hundred head of live cows in the whole of the valley."

He sat down slowly as if his big legs would no longer sustain his weight. "All dead. All ruined. And I might at least have saved a hundred head if I'd driven with you." He lowered his head as if he could not bear the thought. Tolliver and Shorty stared blankly at each other in appalled silence.

CHAPTER 18

RACE PERKINS rose at five o'clock as was her habit, and quitting the living quarters behind the restaurant, built the fire in the big kitchen range. At six-thirty she began serving the first breakfasts, busying herself purposely to try to keep from thinking about what had happened.

The men at the counter were discussing the catastrophe which had overwhelmed the valley. It seemed to Grace that nothing except dead cattle had been mentioned since the tragic ice storm. But her mind, as she turned the browning hot cakes and fried the eggs, was not on the dead cows. She was thinking of Owen Tolliver and his crew, buried somewhere in the frozen hills.

She remembered well the night Porine had ridden in to report that he had left Mac at DeChute's, suffering from pneumonia. The town had been excited then. The doctor had gotten out his sleigh and driven to DeChute's, and Porine had moved on up to the hotel to report to Martha Martel.

Grace had waited then, knowing that afterward the hungry man would seek the restaurant, containing her impatience and anxiety with difficulty.

And he had come, and while he ate he told her of the snow-clogged pass and of the vain wait for help from the Indians, and of finding Johnny Short Bear's frozen body.

She had felt a sharp pang of grief then, for she recalled how the Indian boy had looked, eating at the kitchen table, and the confident way he had started north to tell his people that help was on the way.

"Owen's a fool," Porine was saying. He did not realize that it was partly his conscience talking, that he was trying to justify himself in the eyes of this town for having run away. "A fool. Even if he succeeds in snow-shoeing over those mountains I doubt if the Indians can get those cattle through."

She had been serving his pie, and she asked in a strained voice, "You mean that there's a chance he won't get through the mountains?"

"The Indian didn't make it," Porine reminded her, "and Owen wasn't in good shape when he started."

She thought about this after the man left, while she and her mother were washing dishes, and finally without a word she turned and picked up her shawl and threw it over her head.

Her mother looked around quickly. "Where are you going?"

"To the hotel." She offered no explanation, but leaving the restaurant moved quickly up the windy, empty street. It was snowing so heavily that she could not see the hotel doorway until she had almost reached the building.

She came up onto the porch, and kicked the snow from her overshoes and shook out the shawl to remove its white, clinging covering, and afterward came into the welcome warmth of the lobby.

She stopped, held for an instant by genuine surprise as she saw that the place was deserted save for Martha Martel and Bryan Hall. They were sitting in the cane-backed chairs in the far corner, and neither had looked up at the sound of the door.

She stood undecided, then advanced slowly toward them as Hall said, "There's nothing at all you can do, Martha, the herd is lost. It was lost as soon as Tolliver started."

Grace did not wait for the girl's reply. She came forward saying, "At this time I don't believe we should be thinking about the herd. What about the men with it?"

They both turned to look at her and Bryan Hall came slowly to his feet, a shade of annoyance on his good looking face.

"Grace, what are you doing here?"

She said, "Porine was just in the restaurant. He told me that Owen Tolliver tried to snowshoe into the reservation for help, and he doubts that Owen can make it." As she spoke her eyes were on the other girl's face.

Martha Martel's eyes were unreadable. "And just what do you think we can do about it?"

"We can start a rescue party north. Surely some of the men around here would be willing to ride."

The banker said, "Owen pretty well antagonized everyone in the valley. I'm not so sure. I'm not even certain that I would like asking them."

The look Grace gave Bryan Hall froze him into silence. "I'll ask them," she said, "if neither of you will."

"Wait a minute," Martha Martel had risen. "She may be right, Bryan. If we can find some men to ride north we might still stand a chance of saving a part of the herd."

Grace Perkins opened her mouth to protest that she had no interest in saving the herd, that she was thinking of the men. Then she didn't. It did not matter why the rescue party rode out, as long as they rode.

But they did not ride, for before morning the snow had tuned to an icy sleet which was driven before the howling wind like a million tiny bullets.

No man or horse could have faced the blizzard. For three days it raged, crusting the town in a cocoon of three to four inches of ice. Then it snowed again for twenty-four hours, and afterward the sleet came down. The thermometer went to ten below, to twenty, to twenty-five. It was the coldest anyone had ever seen it in the valley, and when the storm finally ceased and the sun came out to sparkle on the ice, it sparkled on a world which death had claimed.

The men rode, searching for drifted stock. They found them all along the eastern rim, where they had moved before the wind, some standing, some buried in the drifts, all dead.

The country was paralyzed. No one could think of anything except the staggering loss. The wealth of the valley was gone. Herds which the owners had struggled for years to increase had been wiped out.

Bryan Hall drove Martha Martel out to the ranch in his cutter. Grace Perkins watched them leave town, the horses rough-shod for the icy trip, moving out warily on the slippery footing. They came back after dark, and came into the restaurant to eat, since Mrs. Knowles at the hotel had come down with pleurisy and was not serving meals.

Grace waited on them, and she was shocked at the tight set of Martha's face. She asked a question and heard the other girl say in a dead voice, "It's all gone. There isn't a living head on the Box M. Even the horses drifted, since there was no one there."

Grace did not know what to say. She spoke to Bryan rather than to the girl. "What about sending some men up the canyon to look for Owen?"

They both stared at her and Martha said shortly, "If Owen had stayed at home where he belonged he might have saved some of the herd." Her tone was flat, final, and Grace moved away, knowing in her heart that there would be no search for Tolliver. But she did not stop trying. She intercepted the banker on his way back from the hotel to the Star, drawing him unwillingly into the shelter of the empty restaurant.

She said evenly then, trying to keep any feeling out of her voice, "I know you don't like Owen, but I'm asking you as a personal favor to me to send some men up to the pass to find out what happened."

He looked at her coldly. "Just why should you be so concerned for Owen Tolliver?"

She flared at him. "I'd be as concerned if it were anyone. I don't understand you at all, Bryan. I guess I never really understood you."

His lips tightened until the skin about his clenched mouth took on a whitish look. "Listen, Grace. I don't think you quite realize what has happened. This valley has lost everything, everything, do you understand? The whole place is ruined."

She was studying him. "But you owned no cattle."

He made a little sweeping gesture with his hands. "You don't comprehend much about business, do you? I run the bank, and my bank has made cattle loans to nearly everyone in the valley. We have loaned more money than the bank actually has."

She frowned. "But how can you do that?"

He said, "Banks borrow money as well as loan it. I make cattle loans, and then I use the paper I acquire on these loans to get a loan from another, larger bank. I pay five percent for the money I borrow and get seven percent from the ranchers. As long as they had cattle, the paper I gave as security for the loans was good. Now that the cattle are dead, it isn't."

She was staring at him. "And what do you mean to do?"

"I don't know." He turned then without further word and left the building, and she watched him through the window as he crossed and went into the saloon.

It was three days later when Shorty rode his weary horse into the livery and walked back on stiffened legs to the restaurant.

The news of his arrival spread across the town like wildfire, for he had told the hostler at the stable that he needed the doctor and that the full crew was safe.

Grace looked at him when he came in, hardly believing her eyes. "Weren't you with Owen Tolliver?"

He nodded, sinking tiredly onto a stool.

She was almost afraid to ask the next question. "Where is he?"

Shorty explained then. The cook was hurt, the Cantwines had stayed with him at Brady's while he and Owen had ridden out for help. "Owen got a sled at Walters' and went back after the cook." He ended as Grace's mother brought forward his steaming breakfast. "I'm to take the doctor back and meet them at Walters'."

He broke off, for the door behind him had opened and Martha Martel came in, followed by Bryan Hall. She walked directly to the counter and slipped into the seat beside Shorty.

"You should have come and told me first."

He looked at her with weary eyes. "I was coming, as soon as I got some coffee."

"The cattle?" She said. "What happened to the herd?"

"At the reservation. The Indians got them up through the Cut. We lost a few along the way, not many."

She took a deep breath, like a person who had been drowning and suddenly finds herself free of the water. "And the money? Owen got paid, didn't he?"

Shorty had his mouth full. He nodded. "It was too heavy to carry. We left it at Brady's. Owen will bring it in on the sled."

Martha Martel had known Shorty for years and had never paid any attention to him. At the moment he was dirty and bearded and unkempt, but she leaned over and kissed him impulsively. "You're a darling," she told the startled rider. "I love you, I love you all."

The room behind her had been filling gradually with townspeople. Someone laughed, some started to cheer. For an instant they forgot that the valley had lost everything it owned, that the money for the Box M herd was about the only money they would see for a long time.

The doctor came in to talk to Shorty. The livery

176

hostler was getting the sleigh ready, the crowd broke up and Martha Martel left, with Bryan Hall still trailing her.

Grace said to the doctor suddenly, "I'm going with you."

Both he and Shorty turned to stare at her.

"There's no woman at Walters'," she said. "You'll need someone to help, someone to act as nurse."

Shorty made his protest. "It's thirty miles to Walters', ma'am, and it's cold and the road is bad. I had to get a fresh horse both at Hemstead's and at DeChute's."

She did not listen. She was already talking to her mother, deciding what food to put up, what things to send. Then they were on the road, the doctor driving the fresh team, Grace at his side, a hot brick beneath her feet while Shorty, rolled in blankets, slept in the rear seat.

It was cold, but the sun was banked by sheltering clouds and there was no glare. They made good time, and still it was three hours before they reached DeChute's, and the sky in the north was more ominous.

DeChute wanted them to stop, but Grace Perkins argued with the doctor until he agreed to push on, and with fresh horses they started for Hemstead's.

Darkness caught them at Cloud's Crossing, and as they came up the steep bank on the far side it was beginning to snow. The doctor urged the team forward. He was a middle-aged man who had spent most of his life in the valley and was used to long calls in all kinds of weather, but as the snow increased and the wind came up he was frankly worried.

Shorty was awake, still in the rear seat of the sleigh, grumbling to himself. "If we lose the road we're finished." But they did not lose the road, and they came into Hemstead's shortly after midnight, so chilled that it was hard for them to walk from the barn across to the house.

They were on the road again before daylight. The snow had stopped and they made Walters' by ten o'clock to find that Tolliver had not yet returned from the meadow with the cook.

They argued then, both Walters and the doctor saying that Tolliver had probably been caught in last night's snow and laid over at Pattons', and that he should be in by noon.

But Shorty and the girl insisted that they push on, and after much grumbling Walters caught up fresh horses and saddled one for himself and rode with them.

They made the eleven miles to Pattons' in four hours, and there was no sign of Tolliver or that he had been there. It looked like more snow, and it was another twelve miles to Brady's. Walters suggested that he and Shorty take the horses and try to get through while the girl and the doctor waited at Pattons'.

Grace Perkins looked at him. "We've come this far," she said, "isn't it a little silly that we don't go on? Something's happened or Owen would have met us before now. Maybe he's hurt. If he is, the doctor will be needed there, not here."

They went on, and the snow held off although the

wind came up with cruel force. The horses were more tired now and they did not like the wind, and their speed decreased. It got dark before they had covered half the distance, and it was nearing midnight again when the darker shape of the Brady buildings rose up out of the night.

There was no light, no smell of smoke in the air, and the fresh snow was untracked as they turned into the yard. They pulled directly up to the house and Walters' hail would have waked the soundest sleeper, but they had no answer. He got down stiffly and thrust open the door, and they heard him strike a friction match.

The doctor was helping Grace from the sleigh when the ranch man reappeared. "Don't come in yet," he told her.

"What is it?"

He hesitated for a moment. "The cook's dead," he said, "and Owen Tolliver isn't here."

CHAPTER 19

DRIVING THE WALTERS' SLED and leading two saddle horses for the Cantwines, Owen Tolliver turned into the Brady yard. It was long after dark and he was not surprised that no lights showed from the old cabin, but neither was there the smell of wood smoke in the frosty air and he knew a quick unease.

He pulled the tired team close to the house door, and got stiffly down, and thrust the door open, calling Ray Cantwine's name as he did so.

There was no sound from within, and no heat came out through the doorway to greet him. With fingers stiff and claw-like he fumbled in his pocket, found and lit a match, and saw the glint of the lamp chimney in the tiny glow, and moving across, lifted the chimney and put the dying match against the charred wick. It was too far gone and the flame died, and he cursed in the sudden darkness, so tired that he felt the effort of finding and lighting a second match was almost beyond him.

But somehow he worked his stiff fingers back into his pocket, and got a second match and struck it on the table edge and lighted the lamp, screwing up the wick and setting the chimney in its place before he turned to look around the bare room.

Only then did he see the cook on the floor and dully wondered why the man would lie there without a blanket to protect him, and then saw the bullet hole, just above the old man's flattened nose, and the dried blood where it had run down and hardened across the floor.

For a moment he was motionless, unbelieving, thinking that his over-strained nerves were playing tricks upon him. Then his head cleared and he was at once alert, and a great, all-consuming anger built up within him as he looked quickly around the rest of the room before crossing to where the cook lay.

The man's gun, an old styled single-action forty-four, was close to the gnarled hand as if the cook had been drawing it when the shot that killed him came.

Aside from the body the room was empty. All but two of the blankets which they had carried from the reservation were missing. The food was gone, so was the coffee pot and the small frying pan.

And the gold. It seemed afterward to Tolliver that it took him a long time to think about the gold, but when he did he suddenly recalled Ray Cantwine's smile and the way the man had said, "Would you leave the gold with me if there wasn't snow outside, Friend Owen?"

Tolliver cursed softly under his breath. He had killed the cook by leaving the gold in this cabin, killed him as certainly as if his own finger had squeezed the trigger.

Mechanically he turned to the stove, and laid a fire and lighted it, and then looked back at the table and saw something which had escaped his attention. Someone had taken a piece of charcoal from the ashes and scratched a message on the table top. He bent over and read:

"Sorry, the old fool wasn't reasonable. He pulled his gun."

There was no signature, but the words and the silent body made the message plain enough. The Cantwines had started to leave with the gold. They should have disarmed the old man first. Perhaps they had not realized that he wore a gun, tucked into the waistband of his trousers as he had always worn it.

He had tried to stop them, and one of the men had shot him, and they had left him where he fell.

Tolliver stared down at the crude, smeared words, and then stonily he went back into the night and drove the sled to the barn and stalled the led horses and the tired team in its doubtful shelter.

Afterward he came back to find the room already fairly warm, and rolled himself in his blankets and stretched out on the hard bunk.

He was almost at once asleep. Years of training and his utter exhaustion combined to wipe his problems from his mind, but that same training roused him before daylight.

The fire had gone out, and the stove was nearly cold. He rebuilt it, not even glancing at the cook's body, then he went out to get food he had brought on the sled, since the Cantwines had cleared out the cabin.

He cooked breakfast, then returned to the barn, breaking the ice in the trough and finding enough water to service the horses.

He picked the best of the led horses and saddled it, then went back to the cabin to make up a small package of food which he tied behind his saddle. He had no rifle and wished for one. Then he mounted, leaving the other horses in the barn, and rode out, following the tracks which the snow webs had made as the Cantwines struck away to the southeast, ignoring the road.

The tracks had drifted slightly but were still clearly visible, since it had not snowed since the men's departure, and he rode steadily, grimly through the morning, thankful that the ice crust beneath its six inch snow covering was strong enough to support his horse.

He made good time, pressing the animal now, for from the direction of the tracks he guessed that the men he followed were headed for Terrill's place below the east rim, and he came into Terrill's yard just before noon, and saw the house door open and was at once alert, the gun in his hand.

But it was only Terrill, followed by his wife, staring at him from the low porch.

"Seen Ray Cantwine?"

"I've seen him," said Terrill, and there was deep anger in his voice. "They stayed here last night, the thieving robbers. They walked in here with a wild story about the trouble you had had with the herd, and how you and the rest of the crew had stayed on the reservation while they broke through on snowshoes. I believed them. We fed them, and gave them our own bed, and in the morning they robbed us. They took my three horses and my rifle and what food they wanted. As they rode out they called that you'd probably be along, hunting them and to tell you that you wouldn't catch them because they were headed over the east rim to Aspen, that they'd be in Mexico if you cared to look them up."

Tolliver listened in silence, his eyes scanning the distant snowy hills. "Did they take snowshoes with them?"

"They did," said Terrill. "I guess they mean to ride in as far as they can and go on over by foot. Why are they running, Owen?"

"For thirty pounds of gold," Tolliver said. "Some men will try a lot for that much money." He got down then and came into the two-roomed house, and drank hot coffee and listened as Terrill continued to curse the Cantwines and the weather.

"Without the horses I'm afoot," Terrill told him. "Otherwise I'd ride with you. I'd like nothing better than a crack at the crawling thieves. How'd they manage to get away from you with the gold?"

Tolliver told him what had happened, and how he had found the old cook dead on the cabin floor. "You haven't got another rifle you could let me have?"

"I haven't. They even walked off with my short gun, damn them, and all my shells. But it's the horses that put us in a spot. I was going to take the woman into town as soon as the roads are fit. There's no use staying here. All our stock are winter-killed."

Tolliver had a second cup of coffee before he rode away. The tracks led onward toward the eastern hills. Maybe the Cantwines did plan to cross the mountains toward Aspen, but he was not sure.

Ray, he thought, was a shrewd and careful man, and Ray must have thought of the gold as soon as he heard of the drive toward the reservation. It explained many things. It explained why he had refused to take back his twenty cows, and why he had volunteered to accompany the herd when no one else in the valley would.

Ray Cantwine had been gambling. He had gambled that somehow they would get through, and that if they did he would have an opportunity to steal the resulting gold and make his way out of the country.

And things could not have worked out better for Cantwine. They had nearly a full day start, they had fresh horses and food and a rifle, and they knew the eastern hills as few men in the valley did. But were they meaning to get out of the valley to the east, or did they have some other plan for escape?

He studied the sky, noting the clouds banking again in the north. A heavy snowfall would blot out the Cantwines' tracks very shortly.

He needed help. He needed to alert the whole valley for the hunt. He needed to dispatch riders to each of the towns along the railroads in an effort to head them off. His best bet was not to follow the tracks but to head directly for Benton and help.

The easiest way out of the valley during the winter months was south along the stage road which led out through Daylight Pass to Cap Rock on the main line of the Pacific Railroad. There was a road to the east and the Cantwines might make it out on snowshoes, but certainly not on horses, and another road led westward past the Walters place and on over the mountain wall toward Dorchester. This would also be filled with snow, and there was no railroad at Dorchester, but a main stage line ran south to connect with the trains at Mountain Springs.

But if they were going south or west, why did they continue almost directly east? Perhaps they meant to reach the line of hills and then turn south, following the lower benches behind their own ranch and Grover's and the Box M until they had made a half circle, bypassing Benton to reach the main trail close to the mouth of the southern pass.

He debated. They would need to avoid all the bigger ranches, and would have to travel a good twenty or thirty miles out of their way. He could follow them, or he could cut directly southwest toward town, pick up what help he could and fan out in an effort to locate the fleeing men.

He made his choice. If he guessed wrong, if they were actually planning to scale the eastern rim, he would lose them altogether, but it was a gamble he felt was worth taking.

As it was he was a long way behind them, and he had no snowshoes. He could hardly hope to catch up with them by following a trail which might be obliterated within two or three hours.

He turned south and rode as directly toward Benton as he could. In the late afternoon he was east of Walters' ranch and he angled across, meaning to strike the main road somewhere between Walters' and Hemstead's. It was beginning to snow, and it would soon be dark, and he hoped to make the road before darkness blanketed him entirely.

And then he struck the tracks of two riders, and swung down to examine them in the fading light. They were sharp and clear, snowed in hardly at all and he judged that they had been made less than half an hour before.

He stood for a long moment, staring down at the

marks of passage and then westward toward where the flying snow obliterated the shadow of the mountains.

The tracks came out of the east, directly behind him, and headed toward the pass behind Walters' ranch and he felt a surge of inner excitement. They might of course have been made by anyone, but as he stood there he had the certain feeling that they had been made by the fleeing Cantwines.

The hunch rode him as he swung back up into the saddle. There would be few stray riders out in this weather, and there was no ranchhouse in the direction from which the tracks came, and they were heading straight west, not swerving north as they would naturally have done, had they been heading for Walters', or south had they been heading for Hemstead's.

He rode forward, thankful for his luck. Had he stayed with the Cantwine trail it would have carried him in a wide circle along the base of the eastern hills until they turned and cut squarely across the valley. He would have been a good twelve hours behind them and with the gathering storm the tracks would have been lost long before Ray and his brother turned back west.

Now he was less than an hour behind them, and as he pressed forward his conviction that this was indeed the trail left by the fleeing men strengthened, for they crossed the main north-south road almost squarely between Hemstead's and Walters' and headed on west, picking up the side trail which branched off toward Walters' summer line camp and the pass beyond.

No valley rider would have any legitimate reason for

following this trail during the winter. The west pass would be snowed full and the line camp not in use.

But the side trail helped, for Tolliver pushed ahead with renewed confidence, no longer struggling to follow the marks of passage which the snow and darkness nearly obscured.

It did not enter his head to turn back to one of the ranches in search of help. Time was important now. If he could catch the Cantwines before they abandoned their horses and pushed up through the snowy mountains on foot he would take his chances with them. And he felt that he had the advantage of surprise. They would not expect that he would be so close behind them.

The trail wound up to follow the bottom of a shallow gully, and the wind was almost directly at his back so that the snow was not driven into his face.

He had lost all conception of time. He was chilled to the bone, and both his hands and feet were numb. He wondered how much longer he could manage to stay in the saddle, how much further ahead his quarry was, and then through the curtain of sifting snow he saw a light gleam for an instant.

He thought that his weary eyes were playing him tricks, and then the light showed again and he realized that he was approaching the Walters' line camp, that the Cantwines must have paused there to rest, sheltered from the storm.

He rode his tired horse forward at a walk. The snow blotted the light again and yet again until he was within a hundred yards of the crude building.

He saw the leanto beside the shack and guessed that the Cantwines had sheltered their animals within and circled to come upwind so that the stabled animals might not scent his mount and give a nickered warning.

He dismounted beside the line of a ruined corral and tied his animal to one of the ancient posts, and flexed his hands to try and bring back their circulation, and then removed his right glove and drew his gun.

He moved forward finally. The shack was old and beaten and Walters did not trouble to keep it in much repair. The single window was broken and someone had stretched a blanket to keep out the cold and snow, but light came through the chinks between the ill-set logs and he came close to the wall to peer through one of these cracks.

Charley Cantwine was beyond the stove, sitting on a box-like chair while Ray got supper on the rusted stove. The smell of boiling coffee and frying meat reached Tolliver and made him weak, sending a sharp, knife-keen pain through the pit of his empty belly.

For a moment he was forced to press his gloved hand against the rough wall for support, then looked again to make certain that both Cantwines had their backs to the door. Then he made his careful way around the corner of the building.

There was a wooden latch. He lifted it gently with his left hand, still gloved. His right was bare, gripping the cold metal of the gun. Then he thrust the door inward, stepping through the opening, saying in a voice that had a cracked sound, even to his own ears,

"Don't move, either of you."

CHAPTER 20

BRYAN HALL watched the doctor and Grace Perkins drive out of town, then turned away from the bank window feeling angry and dissatisfied, and looked up to find Gilbert North the teller watching him, and spoke sharply to the man without remembering exactly what he said.

Afterward he moved back to his desk and sank heavily into the chair and for long moments sat motionless, his shoulders hunched, his big body utterly slack. Anyone watching might have assumed that he was asleep with his eyes open, but Bryan Hall had never been more alert.

His active mind was trying to readjust his position to the current happenings and he did not find the picture pleasing. Until the killing ice storm had wiped out most of the stock, the future of the valley had seemed very bright, but in a few tragic days everything that so many had worked for had been swept away.

Hall had no way of knowing how wide a territory had been struck by the storm. He did not realize that the condition, instead of being local affected the entire northwestern portion of the country from the Great Plains to the Rockies. This in fact was the year of the *BIG DIE*. That was the way men later referred to it, and nearly every rancher north of Texas had been wiped out.

No other winter storm in history was so widespread, none had lasted longer, or come with more violence. It had howled down from the north bringing recurrent snows which continued to fall intermittently for over forty days, capped by the worst ice storm the frontier had ever known.

On the open plains cattle had drifted before its screaming fury until they starved or until they froze to death, caught against some drift fence, or some rocky line of hills. The cold had been excessive, almost unbelievable.

The valley itself did not suffer to the same extent as did the ranchers on the unbroken plains, for the circling hills had given a degree of protection, but they had suffered enough. The winter set the country and the cattle business back a good ten years. In places, cattle never returned but the land was taken over by wheat farmers. It brought bank failures and hardship clear across the West. It was one of the great catastrophes in history.

But Bryan Hall neither knew nor cared about the rest of the country. His selfish interest was centered on the valley and the bank, and his active mind was wrestling with the problem of how best to turn the situation to his own advantage.

The Benton bank, like all small banks, was in a precarious position. No small institution has sufficient capital and deposits to be able to make all the loans which its customers want. To meet this need all small banks borrow from larger institutions, rediscounting their commercial paper for such loans. In the case of the Benton bank, Bryan Hall had made loans to more than half the ranchers in the valley, taking chattel mortgages on their cattle as security. He had in turn, taken these chattel mortgages and borrowed on them from Burton Glass of the Territorial Land Bank in Cap Rock. Ordinarily his loans from the larger bank would not be due to be paid until after the fall roundup. But now the cattle, on which his mortgages were based, were dead, and undoubtedly the Land Bank would call its loans.

Something had to be done. The capital paid in by stockholders of the Benton bank was only thirty thousand dollars. Added to this the bank had deposits which were near the twenty thousand mark. A fifty thousand dollar total, and yet the Benton bank had loaned over sixty thousand on cattle which were now dead. Simple arithmetic would show anyone the hopeless position they were in, and yet, with luck there was a way out. Owen Tolliver was bringing in eight thousand dollars in gold.

Bryan Hall smiled to himself. He had to see Martha at once. If he handled this properly he might find himself in control of the whole valley, for he had not only taken chattel mortgages on the stock. He had also secured their position by taking mortgages on the land itself, and these he had held, not passing them on to the Cap Rock bank.

He entered the hotel, and climbed the stairs and knocked on the girl's door and heard her stir within, and then she called, asking who it was. He told her, and there was a marked pause before the door opened and she was facing him.

"I've got to talk to you. It's tremendously important." He kept his voice low. There might be someone in the adjoining room and the building's walls were thin.

She hesitated. "I'll meet you in the lobby in five minutes."

That did not please him. He would have preferred to talk with her in the privacy of her room, but he knew her well enough not to argue.

"It's this way," he said when they were finally seated in the corner of the empty lobby. "The valley lost ninety percent of its cattle in the recent storm. The small outfits fared better than the larger ones because they only had a few head to care for. In some cases they brought calves into the houses."

She looked at him, wordlessly, and he went on. "You were lucky. Although you lost your breeding stock and calves Tolliver got most of your beef animals over the pass and got paid for them."

Still she did not speak. She had her father's ability to listen, to make the other person take the lead. It irritated Bryan Hall that her face was so hard to read, that it was difficult to guess what she was thinking about. A little of this irritation crept into his voice when he added,

"So, because Owen Tolliver is a stubborn fool, because he practically stole your herd, you come out in comfortable circumstances while the rest of the valley is ruined."

She nodded, and he said almost harshly, "Can't you talk? Haven't you anything to say?"

"What do you want me to say?" She was unhurried, probing him with her eyes. "You came to talk to me. I'm waiting to find out what is on your mind."

"Can't you guess?" He was reluctant to expose his hand until she gave him some lead.

"I don't like guessing." Her words were crisp. "What do you want, Bryan? What do you hope to gain?"

"What makes you think that I hope to gain anything?"

She smiled faintly, without mirth. "I know you rather well, Bryan."

"Do you?" This was not exactly the opening he had been hoping for but he realized that it would have to do.

"I think so. You have always managed to keep your eye on the main chance. I think the reason I decided not to marry you is that in a great many ways we are much alike, so alike that I would not risk it. One family can not stand two leaders."

He accepted this for the moment without argument. "We are alike. That is the reason I'm here. It's only fair that you be told that there is a fair chance that the bank may fail."

She was instantly alert, all pretense of disinterest

gone. "Fail?"

He nodded. "We owe the Territorial Land Bank at Cap Rock about twenty-five thousand dollars. We discounted that much paper with them and put up cattle mortgages we hold as security. Since the cattle are dead, and the mortgages therefore worthless, they very probably will call our loan."

"But . . ."

He shrugged. "If the bank fails the holders of capital stock under the law are liable for one dollar assessment for every dollar's worth of stock they hold. You are the majority stockholder. It would wipe out all your deposit and most of the eight thousand Owen is so fortunately bringing back to you."

She was gasping, not quite ready to believe him fully and yet knowing that he must be telling the truth.

"But what can we do?"

He said, "Several things. Fortunately over half the money on deposit at the bank belongs to the Box M, and you are about the only stockholder in the whole bank who could stand an assessment.

"First, therefore, we make a deal with Mr. Glass at the Territorial Land Bank. We pay off part of his loan with what money the bank has on hand. We then get him to take your personal note on the balance. I know I can arrange it when he understands that after the reorganization you will in effect be the bank."

She didn't answer.

"Next we assess every stockholder. We can take what deposit credit they have at the bank against such assessments, which means that we will not have to meet any heavy withdrawals. Those who can't pay, and I can give you a list from what I know about their business, will simply lose their stock, which will revert to the bank. From owning about sixty percent as you do now, your percentage will rise to nearly eighty-five, perhaps even ninety. We can probably buy the other stockholders out at a very reasonable figure as they are bound to be short of cash. In effect, the bank will belong to you."

She did not try to conceal her bewilderment. "But what good will it be if it's ruined?"

He smiled at her. He had the heady feeling of being finally appreciated. He said, "But it's not ruined, at least not in the way you mean. When I gave those cattle loans, I took secondary mortgages on the ranches themselves. I did not turn this land paper over to the Cap Rock bank.

"We will levy on the chattel mortgages, get deficiency judgments and then foreclose on the ranches. Inside of six months the bank will own three-quarters of this valley, and you will own the bank. With the land as collateral we'll have no difficulty getting outside loans to restock the valley, or if we prefer we could probably sell the whole place to one of these foreign syndicates who are coming into the American cattle business."

She was staring at him. She did not question that what he said was true. She had enough respect for his shrewdness to believe him. Her busy mind was turning over the possibilities which he had outlined.

The valley had originally belonged to her father, and she had always resented the fact that he had given a good part of it away. Yes, it would be nice if the Box M filled the valley, if her steers ran from one mountain range to the other.

She said, slowly, "And just where do you figure yourself in that, Bryan? Where do you get your share?"

He did not like the sharpness of her tone, but he told her, smiling, "All this will take a lot of handling by someone who understands banks and bankers and loans. You need me. It would be far simpler if you married me. I've never stopped loving you."

She dismissed this with a little impatient gesture.

He hid his disappointment. He had waited a long time. He could wait longer. He could so involve her affairs that she would not be able to do without him.

He said, "I'm sorry. I chose a poor time to remention my suit. I still love you, no matter how you feel, and my one real desire is to help you. You can decide how much that help is worth. You can decide once we have the bank and valley safely in our grasp what my help has been worth to you."

She said, "Bryan, don't get hypocritical. I told you before that I know you too well. Even now I'll bet that I can guess what you are thinking. You are thinking that you will complicate things to the point that unless I make a deal that you like you will see that I never get straightened out."

He was suddenly angry, it was almost as if this girl

could read his innermost thoughts. He felt suddenly that he hated her, but he controlled himself.

He said with painful clearness, "What does that mean?"

"That I don't trust you," she said. "You have a devious mind, Bryan. The first thing you thought of after the storm hit was how to turn the situation to your own advantage."

He let something of his feelings show as he sneered. "Don't try to make me believe that you are feeling sorry for your poor neighbors who got winter-killed. The only thing in this world that has ever interested you is in taking care of yourself."

She nodded. "That's right." Her tone was as hard as his.

"Then why criticize me?"

"I'm not criticizing. I'm merely saying that I never intend to give you the chance to do to me what you are planning that we will do to others."

He lost the rest of his restraint, saying savagely, "So you intend to use my plan to take the valley, and freeze me out entirely?"

"I'm not certain yet what I intend to do. I may even keep you at the bank, and give you a chance to make something for yourself, but if I do, I'll watch every move you make."

For a moment his anger was so great that he could not speak. When he mastered himself he told her, "You are Joe John's daughter, and all your life things have come your way, but that doesn't mean that you are necessarily very smart. It doesn't mean that without me you could go ahead and take over the valley. I'll tell you now that unless I'm included I'll see that you don't."

She was watching him, apparently unaffected by his tirade. "And just how could you stop me?"

"Several ways," he told her. "Public opinion for one thing. Supposing I told the ranchers what you are planning to do. They might not lynch you, since you are a woman, but again they might. A lot of them aren't normal now. They're pretty badly upset by losing all their cattle, and if they thought you were going to take their ranches I'd hate to think what they'd try."

She smiled thinly. "I don't think you'll talk to them."

"And why not?"

"Because I'd merely tell them that the plan was yours, and that when I refused to agree you tried to revenge yourself by accusing me. I think they'd believe me, Bryan. They are feeling pretty sold out because they did not send some of their cows on the drive with Owen, and they haven't forgotten that you are the one who advised against it. I don't think they'd listen to you, now that their stock is dead. Except for you they might have been paid a part of the eight thousand Owen is bringing home."

He stared at her. "You were against that drive."

"Was I? How many people know that I was? Don't forget, those were my steers which were driven north, and don't forget that it is my eight thousand which Owen is bringing home. You won't help yourself,

199

talking against Owen or me. If I were in your place I'd keep my head low and my voice down until the valley forgets how very wrong you've been."

She turned then, and moved away from him to climb the stairs, not looking back. He stayed where he was until she disappeared, then quietly he turned and left the lobby, his face blank, drained of everything including hope.

CHAPTER 21

RAY CANTWINE stood motionless, as if he had been carved from stone. His brother did not move or speak. For a long moment the only sound about the room was the crackle of the fire within the old stove and the sizzle of frying meat as it bubbled in the hot grease of the iron pan.

Owen came in and used his left hand to shut the door, saying flatly, "You've got company, Ray," using the phrase the bench rancher had used when they were first gathering the travel herd.

Ray Cantwine chuckled and deliberately laid the fork he held in the skillet, and slowly raised his hands until they were shoulder high as if he wanted to make it absolutely clear to the man beside the door that he had no intention of trying to reach his holstered gun.

Then he turned slowly until he faced Tolliver, his long, thin mouth beneath the curling, unshaved beard sardonic, a little self-mocking. "What are you, Owen, an Indian or a mind reader?"

Tolliver had a momentary admiration for the man. There was no fear in Cantwine, and no whining. He was caught, and that was a part of the game. Then Tolliver remembered the old cook, dead on the floor at Brady's and all sympathy went out of him.

He said, shortly, "I was lucky. I didn't know which way you were headed and it was beginning to snow so I cut away from your trail and headed for Benton. I crossed your tracks by accident and played a hunch."

Cantwine was staring at him. "You couldn't know they were our tracks. The logical thing for us to have done would have been to keep heading east instead of doubling back."

"I figured that was what you wanted me to think. If you said you were headed east, the chances were that you were planning to go another way. Why did you have to do it, Ray?"

Cantwine's expression was difficult to read. "Why is a man the way he is, Owen? Maybe by birth, maybe by chance, maybe because there is something missing inside of him."

"I never understood you." Tolliver moved forward cautiously. "You are smarter than the average and somewhere you picked up an education which is better than most of the people in the valley have. You don't talk like a brush jumper, and you don't act like one."

Cantwine showed a trace of bitterness. "I'd have been better off if I had thought like they do. Most of the small ranchers are content to live out their lives the way the hand is dealt them. I never was. I wanted more than I had, a lot more."

"And to get it you went on the drive with me, figuring from the first to steal the gold?"

"If the opportunity offered."

Tolliver said, "After what you've done, you have no thanks coming, but it's hard to forget that when the rest of the valley turned their backs you went along, and you stuck, even after Porine quit. If you only hadn't killed the cook. He stuck too. I owe him something, maybe more than I owe you. He wasn't after the gold."

"The old fool." Cantwine had almost a note of affection in his voice. "Why did he have to play heroic? Why did he have to have that gun hidden by his coat? If I'd known he had it he'd be alive now. I didn't want to kill him, but when he tried to shoot me I had no choice." It was not a defense, merely a kind of apology.

Tolliver felt that he understood Cantwine better than he ever had before. Cantwine's acts were not prompted by viciousness, but merely by what he considered necessity.

He said, "I'm sorry, Ray. You lower one hand and drop your gun, afterward step back against the wall while Charley unloads his."

Cantwine made no effort to obey. "What do you plan to do, Friend Owen?"

"Take you to Benton."

"I think not," said Ray. "I have no wish to go to Benton. There are two of us and only one of you, and you have been in the saddle a long time. You can't take us through the storm. One of us would slip away before we had covered a mile. Then you would be in deep trouble. You can hold us here until the snow stops, or until weariness forces you to sleep. To me it looks like a standoff. You can't hope to guard us every minute. One false move and you are dead." He was again smiling mockingly, a man who was not afraid, who was willing to take his chances and was therefore dangerous.

Tolliver's voice was flat. "The easy way would be to put a bullet into each of you."

"Which is exactly what I would do if I were in your shoes." Cantwine's smile had widened. "But it is also something impossible for you to do, to shoot down two unarmed men. You have lived by principles all your life, and you can not break those principles now. Be sensible, Owen. Take the gold and ride out. I had no real desire to see you hurt."

"No."

"Then you have a problem, and I am curious as to how you will solve it." He walked forward slowly, his hands still well above the level of his shoulders to show his peaceful intent, and sat on a rickety chair, crossing his legs and smiling up at the man he baited.

"All right, Owen, the move is yours."

Tolliver hesitated for the barest instant. He knew that Cantwine was purposely trying to anger him, trying to make him make a mistake that would give the brothers their chance. He surprised them by suddenly moving sidewise to the wall bunk and sitting down on its edge.

"Charley, that coffee in the pot should be about

ready. Pour a cup and set it on the table."

The older Cantwine looked at him, then at his brother. Ray shrugged. "I guess we can spare him a cupful."

Charley rose. He lifted the blackened pot and poured the heavy liquid into it and set it on the table, then turned back to his seat beside the stove. No one moved.

Ray said, mockingly, "There's your coffee. Aren't you going to drink it?"

Owen nodded. He rose, shifting his gun to his left hand, and moved toward the table. When he was opposite Ray he suddenly jumped, and before the man realized what had happened he had wrenched the heavy gun from Cantwine's holster, spinning away as he did so before Cantwine's lowering hands could catch his shoulder and swinging around so that the guns covered both men.

Charley Cantwine had been caught entirely by surprise and before his slow mind brought his hand swinging toward his own gun he was staring into the muzzles of Tolliver's weapons.

"Don't try it, Charley."

Charley sat frozen, his claw-like fingers only inches from his gun. Owen said, quietly, "Bring it out, slow, and drop it on the floor."

For a bare instant there was a look of purpose in Charley Cantwine's eyes, then they dulled and he obeyed meekly, the heavy gun striking the hard-packed floor with a dull thump.

"Kick it across to me."

Charley kicked, and Tolliver used his own toe to send it sliding further toward the front wall. He followed it, backing across the room, never taking his eyes from the watching men.

He paused, his back to the wall and reaching over with his right hand pulled the door a little open and flung Ray Cantwine's gun through the crack into the snow outside. Afterward he stooped and catching up Charley's weapon repeated the performance.

"Damn you." It was Ray Cantwine, his mask of studied control cracking.

Tolliver kicked the door shut. "That's just to keep you from getting into real trouble, Ray."

Cantwine's tone was bitter. "I'd say we were in real trouble."

"I'd call it that." Tolliver walked to the edge of the table, picked up the coffee cup with his free hand and drank, his eyes watching them above the rim.

The bags of gold were on the far end of the table. Cantwine glanced at them and his tone was more bitter as he added, "I wish you weren't so soft hearted. I wish you'd shoot us and be done with it."

Owen did not answer. The silence in the cabin grew. Outside the wind increased its violence. Cantwine said, finally, "Is there any reason I shouldn't finish getting supper now that my gun is out in the snow?"

"No reason I know of."

The man rose and moved back to the stove. He turned the slowly frying meat, set cups and tin plates on the table and then began to fry up a batch of sourdough. Tolliver had taken a seat at the far end of the table, laying his gun beside the gold sacks. Cantwine filled a plate and shoved it down to him, then refilled his coffee cup.

They ate in silence, disturbed only by the noise of the storm without, beating against the thin door and blanketed window. When they had finished Cantwine sat back, breathing deeply. "Wouldn't have a cigar in your pocket, Friend Owen?"

Tolliver shook his head.

Cantwine sighed. "I wish I'd never thought of that gold. I'd trade it all to step into a saloon and drink one of Baldy's whiskey slings."

Tolliver did not speak and Cantwine stood up. "Might as well get the dishes cleaned up. Mind if I fetch a bucket of snow?"

"I'll get it. Toss over the bucket."

The man shoved the bucket across the table. Tolliver picked up his gun and backed to the door. He opened it and dipped it into the snow bank outside.

Cantwine had turned to the woodbox. He opened the stove door with one hand and bent forward to pick up a stick, straightening, his right hand holding the wood, his left hidden by his body. "Set the bucket on the stove, Owen."

Tolliver was crossing the room. He saw Cantwine pivot suddenly and realized that the man had a gun in his free hand, and with a swinging motion sent the bucket hurling toward Cantwine's head, at the same moment lifting his own gun.

The bucket caught Cantwine in the shoulder, just as his gun exploded, knocking him slightly around so that the bullet struck the single lamp, breaking it into a thousand pieces and flinging burning oil across the table top.

The oil flared and then died to a low, blue flamed flicker which gave little light. Tolliver fired an instant after Cantwine and the bullet struck home. He knew it even before the man went to his knees.

The spots of burning oil on the table top made a slight, bluish radiance, giving the room a weird unearthly quality which turned everything unreal and indistinct.

Ray yelled as he fell, and Tolliver realized that the wounded man was tossing the gun to his brother and pivoted as Charley, on his feet, snatched the gun by its snout from the table where it fell, trying as he did so to reverse it.

Owen shot again, and saw Charley try to steady himself and fail, and slump forward across the table, face down. Tolliver jumped in to knock the weapon away from the useless fingers, and stood for an instant before he decided that the danger was past. Then he turned to set a candle stub from the shelf above the stove and lit it from one of the still flaring oil puddles.

Quickly then he beat out the last flickering blue flames before he bent over Charley. The man was dead, and he turned at once to Ray Cantwine. Ray sat on the floor, his back to a table leg, his arms clasped tightly around his stomach. He looked up at Tolliver and his bearded lips twisted into the ghost of their old mockery, but when he spoke it was in a pain-laden whisper.

"In the belly," he said. "I've seen men die this way and it was no fun. Why didn't you get me in the head?"

Tolliver holstered his gun and bent to have a look.

"No use." The seated man did not remove his arms. "You were quick with that bucket, Friend Owen. I thought I had plenty of time." He coughed and a trace of red foam showed on his lips.

Tolliver wiped it away.

"The woodbox is a good trick," Cantwine said when he could speak. "I saw it used once down on the Rio Grande. I didn't expect you or anyone to show up tonight, but I was ready. At least I thought I was. I always put a gun there from habit."

Tolliver said, "Stop talking until I carry you to the bunk."

"For what? Charley gone?"

Tolliver nodded soberly.

"Just as well, if I'm going to die." The seated man seemed to be staring past Tolliver at something a long way off. "Charley never could get along very well by himself. Nothing wrong with him, just needed someone to make up his mind. Guess I got him into a lot of trouble here and there." He was silent a long moment, then with a long sigh; "Do me a favor, Owen. Give me one last look at that gold."

Tolliver rose and getting the sacks from the end of the table dumped their contents on the floor in front of

Ray Cantwine. The coins looked dull, a little worn in the flickering candle-light.

"Used to dream about gold." The seated man's voice was a whisper. "Used to plan on what I'd do when I had so much gold it wouldn't fit in my pockets. Nearly got it this time." He smiled then, and settled back against the table leg. It was several moments before Owen Tolliver realized that Ray Cantwine was dead.

CHAPTER 22

COMING INTO BENTON shortly after noon Owen Tolliver stabled his tired horse and carrying the two leather bags walked down the street and into the bank.

His progress was marked by real attention as he moved along the snowy way. Half a dozen people stopped him to ask questions and then followed him as far as the bank entrance.

Parkingstead had tried to get the story before he left the livery, but he moved out saying, "later," and then stopped when he met Karl Zeeman outside. The marshal looked at his unshaved cheeks, his wind-burned face and sunken eyes.

"I've seen healthier looking dead men," he said.

Tolliver fell in step. "Send someone out to Walters' line camp after the Cantwines, and someone to Brady's after my cook." He weighed the heavy bags he carried. "Hardly seems that this much gold is worth three men's lives."

"Hardly." Zeeman's tone was dry. He walked at Tolliver's side, hearing a brief outline of the drive and in turn told Owen of the havoc the storm had wrought across the valley.

"Everyone's busted," he said. "The ranchers are having a meeting tonight to talk about it. You'd better come."

Tolliver sighed. He was exhausted. He wanted a bath and a shave and a chance to sleep. They moved on, passing the restaurant and he glanced through the windows.

Seeing the look Zeeman said, "Didn't you meet Grace? She rode out with the doctor."

Owen Tolliver stopped in surprise. "Rode out with the doctor?"

"And Shorty. She figured that your cook might need nursing. She's been taking care of Mac ever since the Pattons brought him in. He's mending nicely, thanks to her."

Tolliver did not comment as they moved on slowly.

"Attractive too." The marshal seemed bound to talk. "I might look in that direction myself if it wasn't for Bryan Hall."

Owen gave him a tired grin. Zeeman had been a determined bachelor for sixty years. "You're a fraud, Karl."

Zeeman pretended vast surprise. "Are you just finding that out?"

Tolliver turned in at the bank door. "Come on with me. I want a witness when I deposit this with Bryan."

Zeeman glanced at him quickly, but Owen's face was expressionless and they went up the bank steps together.

Bryan Hall had been standing before the window, talking to the teller. He turned as they came in, and as he saw Tolliver his eyes darkened with quick anger.

But he controlled himself in an instant and said in his level, neutral voice, "Home, Owen? I hear you had a tough ride."

"A tough ride," Tolliver agreed, and waited for him to stand aside so he could place the gold bags on the high counter.

"Deposit this to the Box M account, all but two hundred. Put that in a separate account until we can find out if the Cantwines left any heirs."

Bryan Hall said quickly, "What happened to the Cantwines?"

Karl Zeeman answered. "They're both dead. They thought they wanted it all." He gestured at the leather bags.

Behind the counter Gilbert North had started to prepare the deposit slips. He stopped, holding his stub pen, staring in surprise. Hall was staring also. Slowly both of them shifted their attention, looking quickly at Owen.

He ignored them, leaning against the counter, the picture of utter weariness, his face a hard mask beneath the uncut beard.

Neither questioned him. After a moment the teller went back to filling out the deposit slips and without a word handed them out to Owen, not even counting the gold.

Tolliver tucked them into his pocket and turning left the building pausing outside to say, "Do me a favor, Karl. Go over to Pettycords and buy me some underwear, socks and a clean shirt. They know my size. Bring them over to the barber shop." He did not wait for an answer but turning, headed for the barbershop.

Here he sank into the single red plush chair, and let Genesee use scissors to cut away the worst of his beard and then lay back with his lathered face under the softening towel, nearly asleep.

The scrape of the razor against his chapped cheeks was painful and the witch hazel was soothing for all its bite. Afterward he carried his bar of soap into the bathroom at the rear and watched Genesee's son fill the single tub with steaming water.

Then he climbed in soaking the grime of the trail and the soreness from his body, too tired to think. Zeeman came in with the fresh clothes and sat by smoking while he dressed, saying,

"The town has not had so much excitement in twenty years. People don't know whether to treat you as a hero, or to be jealous because you earned money for Box M cows while they were losing everything they had."

Tolliver showed no interest.

"I saw Martha on the street. She said to tell you that she would be waiting in the hotel lobby."

This, Tolliver knew, was a command, but he did not

want to talk to anyone at the moment. "I need sleep bad."

Zeeman considered. "If you leave by the front you'll be answering questions the rest of the day. By the back you could reach my office without being seen."

They went out the back door and into the living quarters behind the marshal's office. Zeeman put the coffee to boil and started to make a thick sandwich of cold meat.

Tolliver said, "I'm not hungry."

The marshal finished the sandwich. "Be better with something in your belly." Owen did not argue. He ate part of the sandwich and drank the coffee. Afterward he slept, his senses dulled, almost drugged.

Yet even in sleep he knew a sense of urgency, and he was far from rested when Zeeman shook him at six. "I hate to disturb you, Owen, but Martha is raising hell. I told you about the ranchers' meeting tonight. She says she has to talk to you before it starts."

Tolliver dragged himself into a sitting position, and then managed to stand up. "A law officer could not possibly have whiskey in his home."

Zeeman grinned and fetched a glass and poured a small shot into it, saying, "It's not that I begrudge you a man sized drink, but in your frayed-out condition it could knock your head off, and I think you will need your wits about you before this night is over. It is a hunch I have."

Tolliver did not answer. He sipped the whiskey slowly, feeling its warmth run up through him. He felt that actually his whole body would never be entirely warm again. It was as if the winter's freezing cold had taken up a permanent position in his bones.

He set the glass down. He had a deep reluctance to talk with Martha. It seemed to be growing rather than diminishing as time passed, but there was no help for it.

He left the marshal's office and started toward the hotel, pausing as he came abreast of the lighted windows of the restaurant. On sudden impulse he turned and went in, knowing a keen, quick disappointment when he did not find Grace in the outer room, and then he saw her through the kitchen doorway before the big stove.

There were half a dozen people in the restaurant who looked up with quick interest as he entered. He paid them no attention, moving between the tables and coming through the kitchen door to pause beside the girl.

She had not heard him come. She turned, carrying a hot skillet and stopped in surprise. "Owen."

He took a step forward. "I wanted to thank you for taking care of Mac and for riding out with the doctor."

She set the skillet back on the stove. "It was nothing, but it was a shock, coming into Brady's, not finding you there. Finding the cook."

He said, "I can understand."

They considered each other. Now that he was here Tolliver found it difficult to speak. Something in the room had changed. There was a restraint between

214

them, an embarrassed awareness of each other which had not been present at their earlier meetings.

She said finally, a little nervously, "I heard about the Cantwines. It—it was too bad."

He nodded. He did not want to talk about the Cantwines. He did not even want to think about them. It was something which he would have liked to wash from his memory. He said with awkwardness, "I want to talk to you. There are a number of things I want to say, but the ranchers are having a meeting. I should be there and it may be late before the meeting is over. Will you wait here until I'm through?"

The color had risen in her full cheeks and her eyes questioned him, but she did not pretend to misunderstand his meaning. "Is that wise, Owen?"

"Very wise," he said, knowing that she was referring to Martha.

"Then I'll be waiting." There was no coyness in the words, only a straightforward honesty.

He left the restaurant, relieved, not conscious that every person in the room watched him as he crossed to the door. He had been confused and unhappy when he entered. He was not as he advanced through the snowy night toward the lights of the hotel.

He knew now that he had something which he must tell Martha, something which had grown upon him during the long, chilly nights of the trail. But when he came into the lobby the girl gave him little chance. She seized the initiative as soon as she had led him into a corner and pressed him into the chair.

"If I didn't know better I'd be certain you've been avoiding me."

He had been avoiding her, but he was through avoiding her now. He was ready to tell her, but he said, first, "I was pretty well played out."

She looked at him critically. "I've seen you as bad, after a roundup."

He let this pass.

"And I haven't thanked you for getting the herd through safely. I suppose you expect me to."

He did not answer, and his silence seemed to increase her anger. "Owen, I never could stand a smug person, especially when he has just proved that he was right and I was wrong. Don't be too proud. You couldn't have foreseen the ice storm. You could not have known it would kill all the cattle in the valley."

"Of course I didn't."

"Then don't adopt an *I told you so* attitude with me. It happens that things worked out for the Box M because you refused to listen to what I said, because you forced me to go along. But don't try it again."

He said, wearily, "This whole argument seems senseless to me. What are you trying to prove? There are much more important things to think about at the moment than to worry about your wounded pride."

Her eyes darkened and the flush in her cheeks was danger bright. "Owen."

The blanket of his weariness gave him a blunt courage. "You're full grown, Martha. You aren't a little girl any more to be pampered and petted. You've got to begin to face your responsibilities."

The toe of her small shoe was tapping warningly on the old floor. "What responsibilities are you talking about?"

"To the valley. To the people who have lost everything. Call it luck. Call it what you will, but the Box M is the only ranch which came out of this with anything, and you alone are in a position to help re-establish cattle on this range."

She was staring at him. "Are you out of your mind? Do you expect me to throw in what little I have left to help the very people who refused to help you?"

"It's the only sensible thing to do."

"Sensible." Her tone rose until the other people in the lobby turned to look curiously in their direction.

"Careful." His warning was automatic. He had watched over her for so long.

She glanced around, fighting to control herself, then lowered her voice, saying in a tight whisper, "Listen to me. I'm going to restock this valley, but not for the loafers who have lived off Box M handouts for years. I'm going to restock it for myself, for us."

"You're what?"

"I'm going to take the valley back. Joe John owned most of it once and like a fool gave it away. I'm going to take it back."

He said, slowly, "I don't believe I understand what you are talking about."

"Don't you? I'll tell you then. Pete Daily owes the bank money. So do Walters and Hemstead and Zeigler and the rest. The loans were secured by their cattle. The cattle are dead."

He stared at her.

"In turn," she said, "the bank has borrowed from Mr. Glass of the Territorial Land Bank in Cap Rock. His loans must be repaid or the bank will fail."

He said, "I seem to see Bryan Hall's hand in this."

She laughed. "Bryan told me how it could be done. Bryan thought I'd give him a share, that I might even marry him. But we don't need Bryan. You and I can handle things. You and I can call the loans, foreclose on the mortgages."

He stooped slowly to pick his hat from the floor beside the chair, then stood up. "I'm afraid you'd better count me out on this."

She looked blankly at him, for a moment not quite believing she had heard properly, then her eyes hardened and her mouth was a tight line.

"I'm going to need help on this, Owen."

"Not from me."

She said, angrily, "If not from you, from someone else, from Bryan Hall probably. How would you like it if I married him?"

He gave her a long steady look, then without answering he turned and walked away from her across the lobby. Not until he had stepped outside did he recall that he had not told her what he had gone to the hotel to say, that he loved Grace Perkins, that he meant to marry the girl if she would have him.

CHAPTER 23

BRYAN HALL had spent a miserable day considering his own future. And Tolliver's deposit of the gold from the reservation had not improved his frame of mind.

He was angry with himself and with the world, but mostly with Martha Martel. He had worked hard for the bank and he felt without undue pride that it was his work which had built it into a really going business.

Now, through no fault of his own, that business was near ruin, and his plan to take advantage of the situation had been usurped by Martha. She would foreclose the ranches. She would take over the valley, and if the whim suited her, she would keep him on at the bank, carrying out the details for her for his meager salary.

His mind rebelled at the thought. He watched Tolliver and the marshal leave the bank and then turned to watch Gilbert North place the sacks of gold in the safe.

And the thought came that that gold, plus the other funds which the safe held, would make a comfortable stake with a which a shrewd man might start a new life for himself far from this ruined valley.

He rejected the thought as he walked to his desk and sat down, but it kept recurring to his mind. Martha had turned him down flatly. Martha preferred Owen Tolliver, and together they would rule this valley. But they wouldn't rule it if the money were gone. The land bank would take everything. They would be as broke as the other ranchers.

The thought pleased him, and he knew suddenly that he meant to steal the money from the safe. Once he accepted the decision, his active mind explored the possibilities. He had to get out of town without anyone suspecting he was gone, and he needed as much head start on possible pursuit as he could arrange.

But he dared not touch the safe until after business hours. In fact he would wait until darkness would veil his action, and the loss would not be discovered until tomorrow morning, fourteen or fifteen hours before any hunt would be launched. On a good horse he would be safely through the south pass before then and catch the eleven o'clock train from Cap Rock, dropping off of it before it reached the coast and slipping across the border.

Then he frowned. The meeting of the ranchers was called for that night, and they would expect him there. He debated. Perhaps he had best put off the theft until tomorrow night, but if he did, something unforeseen might happen. It must be tonight. He rose and moved over to the teller's cage, saying to Gilbert North that he thought he had a spell of grippe coming on, that he was going to the hotel, to bed and that he wanted the man to represent him at the ranchers' meeting. Then he bundled himself in his coat and left the bank.

But instead of going to the hotel he moved down to the livery stable where he told Parkingstead that he had to ride out to Hemstead's and that since it was already late in the afternoon he would in all probability spend the night.

He saddled his horse and mounting, circled the town so that Gilbert North would not see him pass the bank window, and left the horse hidden in the old shed behind the hotel. Afterward he went through the deserted kitchen and up to his room.

He packed a few possessions in his saddlebags, knowing that the weight of the money he meant to steal would come close to seventy pounds, and wanting to keep the other weight down as much as possible.

He lifted the belted gun, considering it, and finally placed it on the bureau, beside the saddlebags. Then he lay down on the bed, fully dressed, to wait for darkness.

Later he came down the rear stairs and moved along the silent alley to the bank. He let himself into the still warm room and without lighting a lamp crossed to the safe. He knew where everything was and he emptied it of money, packing the contents into the saddlebags.

With the gold which Owen had deposited there must be close to twenty thousand. He straightened, smiling thinly at the trouble Tolliver had gone to to bring that money home. This, he thought, rounded out his revenge. It satisfied him far more than if he had pulled his gun and killed Owen. At least no one in the valley would ever forget him. Certainly not Martha. To her dying day she would probably regret that she had not struck a bargain with him.

He left the bank and moved back along to the shed behind the hotel and mounting his horse circled again around the town, coming into the south road a good mile beyond Benton's limits. He rode easily, not hurrying, and he did not see Grover in the darkness. The rancher had dismounted to adjust a slipping cinch in the shadow of a clump of aspen where the trail crossed Horse Creek, and he turned to stare after the lone rider, surprised that anyone would be riding away from town on the night of the meeting.

For a moment Grover thought it was Bryan Hall, but in the poor light he could not be certain and he must be mistaken. Certainly Hall would be at the ranchers' meeting.

He finished tightening the strap, mounted and rode on into town. He was already late and by the time he climbed the stairs to the meeting hall the room was well filled. He saw Owen Tolliver across the room, talking to Pete Daily and Daily's son, and Honos Walters, and thought how much change a few short days had wrought. He frowned, wishing deeply that he had let Tolliver take his few cows up the reservation trail.

He was not the only man in the big room who was wishing the same thing. Almost every valley rancher was filled with self-anger that they were not to share in the eight thousand dollars the Box M cows had brought. Even a few dollars would have made a vast difference now.

They hushed as Pete Daily moved to the front of the room and raised his big hands for silence. Standing there, his homely, wind-tanned face grave, almost sullen, Daily said, "You all know why we are here. I don't need to go into details. The valley is flat broke."

He paused as if to give his hearers a chance to digest the finality of his words, then he continued. "Some of us are wasting time regretting what we did not do in the past. That's foolish. The question is, what can we do with the future?"

He turned then and motioned and waited until Owen Tolliver came forward to join him, saying, "This isn't easy. I'm not a man who likes humble pie, nor am I saying that if I had it to do over again I'd send cattle with you on a winter drive. I probably wouldn't. But I am asking you as chairman of the bank board to tell us where we stand. To tell us how much help the bank will give."

Owen looked around. Martha was not in the hall. Martha was not here to face her neighbors. He saw Grace Perkins sitting alone at the far side of the room and knew that she was there because of him and felt a growing warmth, and then forgot her as his mind attacked the problem.

"I wish I could answer you," he told Daily. "I can't. You all know that I sit on the bank's board merely to represent the holdings which once were Joe John's. I have no real say because these holdings do not belong to me. The person who owns them is not here tonight."

They stirred, looking around, and he saw the sharp curiosity in their faces and was surprised to realize that he did not care what they thought.

He went on. "I had hoped that Bryan Hall would be here. He knows more about the bank's condition than anyone else. I can't understand where he is."

Gilbert North stood up and explained that Hall was sick and had asked him to attend the meeting.

Tolliver nodded. "I just got home at noon," he told them. "I slept most of the afternoon and have not had time to actually think this thing out. My idea is that several of us should talk to Mr. Glass of the Territorial Land Bank in Cap Rock, explain the situation, explain our willingness to meet our obligations when we can, and ask for an extension on the loans he has made the Benton bank." He did not tell them of Martha's threat to foreclose on the ranches. He was still trying to think of some way to block her. But he had to tell them something.

"It seems to me that the first step is to find out exactly what each of us owes, to find out what the bank owes in Cap Rock and how much cash our bank has on hand. Since Bryan is sick, maybe Gilbert could bring the bank's books over here."

He nodded to the teller who rose and moved toward the stairs. Owen was not certain what he planned to do. He was in fact, stalling, playing for time, hoping that an idea would come.

But he forgot all this a few minutes later as North came racing up the steps in white-faced excitement to gasp, "The safe is empty. The money is gone."

Everyone was trying to talk at once. It was Honos Walters' bull-like voice which quieted them. "Get Bryan Hall." He shouted. "Someone get Bryan Hall."

It was then that Grover began to understand. He

stood up on a chair, yelling at them in his nervous voice. "I don't think you'll find him. I met him on the south trail a good hour ago."

CHAPTER 24

THE MEN who took the snowswept trail toward Cap Rock were silent and grim-mouthed. Pete Daily had voiced all their thoughts when he cursed softly. "The skunk. To think that I listened to that low-down skunk. I thought he had the interest of the valley at heart, but instead he finishes all of us by stripping the bank. If we ever had a chance to pull out it's gone now."

Honos Walters had sworn at them. "Why waste time talking? Let's ride."

They rode. No one was asked to come. No one thought of staying behind. Zeeman rode at Tolliver's side well back toward the rear of the column. As they pulled out he said, softly, "You should have stayed, Owen. Haven't you had enough riding in the last few weeks?"

Tolliver did not trouble to answer.

Zeeman's voice was musing. "It comes to every man, the time when he reaches the branch in the road. I thought Hall was too smart to choose this path, although I have never trusted him."

Tolliver said, slowly, "He was being pushed, Karl, pushed by ambition. He came to Martha, suggesting that between them they foreclose on the ranches and take over the whole valley. She turned him down."

Zeeman glanced sidewise. "She wasn't at the meeting tonight."

Tolliver did not answer for a full minute. Zeeman was the one man left in the valley he felt free to talk to. He said, soberly, "She turned Hall down. She offered me the deal instead."

"And you wouldn't buy?"

Owen Tolliver shook his head. "I can't understand what has happened to Martha since Joe John's death. She's a different person."

Zeeman who had his own ideas on that score, did not comment. Tolliver waited a moment before he added, "If Bryan Hall had only realized it there was no need for him to steal that money tonight. When I turned Martha down she threatened that she would go to Hall for help. If he had waited . . . everything he wanted might have fallen into his lap."

"That," said Zeeman, "is what I meant by everyone sometime coming to the fork in the road. Each of us at some time has a chance to play it dishonestly. It's then that the weak ones show their weakness." He broke off and they rode in silence.

They stopped at Zeigler's and switched horses, finding that Hall had also changed mounts at the ranch. He switched again at the Daily place, the horse he left in the corral showing signs of hard riding.

"It's the gold he's carrying," Tolliver said. "Dead weight kills a horse faster than a heavy man."

They were gaining, but not rapidly. Hall was still a

full hour ahead of them as they came up into South Pass, but they made good time for the pass was wide, the road fairly open and not too drifted.

They dropped down the far side of the saddle and came out through the twisting foothills as day lightened the eastern sky, dropping off the bench into the level high plateau which stretched away toward Cap Rock.

"There's a train at eleven." Daily was still leading. "It may come before we get there, but we can wire ahead and have him taken off at Randell."

"If the wires aren't down," the son said.

Daily cursed. He had forgotten about the ice storm. None of them knew whether the telegraph line was working or not, and the thought made them press forward more rapidly.

Bryan Hall was hoping that the wires were down. He had considered the possibility even before he removed the money from the bank safe. If they were down he had nothing to worry about. If they weren't, he'd have to leave the train sometime within the next twelve hours, get a horse and strike across country for the border.

He rode into Cap Rock a good hour before train time, left his borrowed horse at the livery and carrying the saddlebags walked the short block to the railroad station.

No one had recognized him, but he knew a great many people in town and he dared not go into the restaurant for fear of seeing someone who might inadvertently ask embarrassing questions. He was experiencing his first real fears as a fugitive. He felt that everyone he passed on the snowy street looked at him with undue interest, as if they knew what the saddlebags contained, as if they could tell that he was a thief.

It was very cold, but he was sweating as he gained the station and came into the small waiting room, heavy with heat and the fumes of improperly burned coal gas.

He crossed to the window, asking for a ticket to El Paso. He would have to change trains at Eldia and he had no intention of going to El Paso. His hands trembled a little as he paid for his ticket and his voice was not quite steady when he said, "I'd like to send a wire."

"Not today," the agent told him, "or tomorrow either. The wire's been down over a week. Lord knows when they'll get it fixed if this weather doesn't break. Trains only started running two days ago."

Bryan thanked him and turned away in relief. At least the telegraph wasn't working. If he got the train, he'd be perfectly safe. He sat down in the corner of the waiting room, half concealed by the stove, nursing the saddlebags on his knee, trying not to attract any attention to himself.

Half a dozen people came in and went out of the waiting room, not even glancing in his direction. He counted the minutes by the slowly ticking wall clock, his stomach muscles getting tighter and tighter as each moment slipped away. And then he heard the train's whistle at the lower bridge, a good mile away. It was coming, coming. He was safe.

He paid no attention to the other sounds around the building. His relief was so great that he did not even turn his head as the rear door opened, letting in the clean, wintry air. His first knowledge that he was caught came when Owen Tolliver spoke.

Tolliver had pushed open the rear door, standing in it, staring about the room, thinking for a moment that it was empty. Then he saw Hall's shoulder around the angle of the stove. He stepped in. Hall's back was to him. Hall was staring at the front window, ready to get to his feet when Tolliver spoke. "Well, Bryan?"

Bryan. Hall came erect as if the bench on which he had been sitting had suddenly turned hot. He spun around, almost hitting the stove with his elbow as he did so, clutching the precious saddlebags to him.

"Tolliver!" He stared at Owen as if the big rider had been a ghost, then he let go the bags with his right hand and dropped it toward his holstered gun.

He might have drawn in time had he been willing to let the money bags slide to the floor, for Tolliver's coat was buttoned over his gun belt and he was nearly as surprised as Hall.

But some deep-rooted instinct made the banker cling to the treasure with his left hand as if he knew that once it slipped from his grasp it was gone forever. The heavy bags hampered him and the gun was only half out of the holster when Tolliver's fist crashed against his jaw.

The force of the blow sent Hall backward to crash

into the overheated stove, knocking its short body from the squat legged base and spilling it on its side so that it rolled, strewing coals clear across the worn floor.

Hall had dropped the saddlebags but had somehow retained his balance. He was still trying to free his gun when Tolliver hit him again. This blow swung him half around, the gun slid from his fingers and clattered to the floor. He jumped after it, coming down on his hands and knees. Tolliver landed on his back, locking one arm about the throat, pulling him away from the fallen gun. They rolled over and over across the track of burning coals, their coats beginning to smolder.

The station agent was shouting hoarsely, trying to get his office door open. The train was braking across the platform with the hiss of escaping steam and the shrill of sliding iron. The front door was nearly ripped from its hinges and Karl Zeeman and Pete Daily burst into the room, followed by the valley ranchers.

It was Zeeman who dragged the struggling men apart, but it was Daily who took immediate charge. He jerked Bryan Hall from the marshal's grasp, holding him by the coat collar and swung him around and thrust him out through the door to the snowy platform.

Tolliver with Zeeman's help was beating out the places where his coat was smoldering from contact with the live coals. "I looked through the window and didn't see him," he said. "But when I got inside I spotted him behind the stove. I was so surprised I called his name before I thought."

Zeeman had stooped to pick up the bags. He weighed

them in his hands. "Feels like it must be all here." They moved toward the door and onto the platform, and not until then did either realize what Daily had in mind.

Already he had shoved Hall to the end of the platform and his son was climbing the telegraph pole, carrying a rope with him. There was quite an audience, the platform was filled with townspeople, the crew, and some of the passengers from the standing train.

As Zeeman and Tolliver paused to stare one of the women passengers said in a hysterical voice, "They're going to hang that man. Isn't someone going to stop them?"

Owen was already running through the crowd, Zeeman behind him, carrying the saddlebags. Young Daily was halfway up the pole. The ranchers heard Tolliver coming and split to let him through, and he was facing Daily and. Honos Walters, saying, sharply, "Don't do it, boys. Don't do it."

Walters' face was flushed. Daily was stubborn. "Keep out of this, Owen. He thought nothing of taking the last cash from the valley, of leaving our wives and kids to starve."

Tolliver looked at Hall. The banker seemed curiously shrunken, his face sharp with fear, his eyes mirroring a desperate appeal. "Don't let them. I'll do anything. I'll go away. I'll . . ."

Tolliver had no time for Hall. Daily was the real leader here. Daily was the one he had to fight. "Pete," he said, "you aren't going to hang him because I won't let you. Because I'll stop it if I have to kill you." His

231

coat was unbuttoned and he let his hand settle to his gun.

Daily was furious. "You're one against twenty, Owen."

"Two," said Zeeman. He had dropped the bags and his guns were in his old hands. "Turn him over to the sheriff here."

"Or let him go." It was Tolliver. "You haven't been hurt by what he tried to do. The money is safe. Put him on that train. What good will it do to hang him? It won't bring your dead cattle back. It won't save your ranches and it will lay on your consciences for the rest of your lives."

The men behind Daily wavered and Tolliver, sensing his advantage pressed it, saying to the two men who held the banker, "Let him go."

They released their grip. Daily tried to jump forward. Zeeman held him steady with his guns. Zeeman had faced crowds before, there was no doubt in anyone's mind that he would shoot if necessary.

"Go on," said Tolliver to the banker who stood uncertainly. "Get aboard that train."

Hall obeyed. He ducked away like a frightened rabbit. Walters started after him and Tolliver's voice was a ringing warning. "Stay where you are, Honos."

The man stopped. They stood thus for a moment in strained, expectant silence, then Daily swung away, saying angrily across his shoulder, "I won't forget this, Owen, not ever."

Tolliver did not answer. The ranchers hesitated, then

leaderless they turned and moved back toward their horses. Zeeman replaced his guns and stooping picked up the saddlebags. Owen was staring at the train which was preparing to move out.

Zeeman said, "Why'd you do it, Owen? Because of his girl?"

Tolliver glanced at him sharply, saying after a moment, "I don't know why I saved him. I didn't even stop to think."

"It's better this way." Zeeman's eyes were on the departing train. "I don't think she ever loved him, but if he had been lynched the memory of it might have stood between you."

It occurred to Tolliver that Zeeman seemed to know almost as much of his thoughts as he knew himself. He did not answer. Instead he turned and led the way out of the station yard.

CHAPTER 25

OWEN TOLLIVER stopped at the bank and placed the contents of the saddlebags in the safe under Gilbert North's watchful eye and told the teller, "You are acting cashier until the board fills Bryan's place. You may well get the job."

He moved on then, up the street toward the hotel. The impromptu posse had gone en masse into the Star, but he knew no desire to join them. They had stayed in Cap Rock over night and he had had twelve hours of sleep which left him fresher and more relaxed than he had been in days.

He came into the lobby and sent McCune's boy up to tell Martha that he was there. The boy returned to say that she would see him in her room and he climbed the stairs slowly, going over in his mind what he meant to say.

Her door was open and he stepped in and for an instant they stood motionless, looking at each other, and he knew none of the old stirrings which had once troubled him. She stepped forward as if she meant to come into his arms, but he avoided her by turning toward the straight-backed chair.

"This won't take long," he said. "You probably already have heard that we recovered the money?"

She nodded. "The story is all over town, how you saved Bryan when Pete Daily would have hung him. Why did you? He betrayed his trust, and me, and the bank . . ."

That was it, he thought. Bryan had betrayed her. That was something she would not forgive. He said, "Hanging, or even putting him in prison would not have helped. The money is safe."

She said, "I can't understand you. If anyone in the valley had the right to be angry with Bryan it was you. He undermined you. He tried to block the cattle drive. He . . ."

Owen stopped her with a gesture. He knew that in the years to come she would cease to remember her part in Hall's actions, and put the full blame for everything that had happened on the banker. He no longer cared what she did, but he had things which must be told.

"I spent yesterday afternoon with Mr. Glass of the Land Bank in Cap Rock. The condition we have here is not local. The killing storm covered most of the West. No one knows the full extent of the damage, but the chances are that better than half of the cattle in the country are dead."

She gasped.

He went on. "I explained the condition our bank is in, that even if we could manage to meet his loans we would have nothing left with which to restock our ranges. He understands. He knows that the whole country is bankrupt, and that the only chance his bank or any bank stands to survive is to help the ranchers get back on their feet. He suggested that we use the cash we have on hand to buy Texas feeders as soon as the trails open up, that we also get a few imported bulls and try to grade up our herds. The bank can furnish new cattle loans and the ranchers can combine to drive the animals they buy north in one herd."

"With my money?" She was staring at him. "The answer is no. No!"

He said, "It's the bank's money, and I'm afraid that you won't have too much to say about it, Martha. I told Mr. Glass how opposed you would probably be. He said to tell you that unless the program he has out-lined is carried out he'll be forced to take over the bank, as he may be forced to take over other small banks in the territory. But he also pointed out that a bank is run by its board of directors, and you are not a member of that board."

She said impatiently, "I have control. I can remove the board."

"Not until the annual meeting and that meeting is not until next fall. There were five board members in the posse. We met with Mr. Glass and as directors voted to accept his terms and receive the loan extensions he offered."

She was staring at him, and the anger was deep in her eyes. "You've done it again, Owen. You've put me into a position of having to agree to something whether I like it or not. You did it once when you gathered my steers and started to drive them to the reservation without my consent. I warned you then never to do that to me again. You have, now."

He said, "In ten years you'll look back on this action and be glad of the part you had in saving the valley."

"Perhaps. I doubt it, but you may be right. But that still does not absolve you for treating me in this way. The decision should be mine, but it was not mine. You forced my hand, and if I kept you on the Box M you would continue forcing my hand whenever something came up on which we did not agree. I won't take that, Owen, from you or from anyone else. You are through."

He nodded. "I expected that. Shorty can take over the running of the ranch and you can bring in your new stock from Texas with the general herd. Even if this had not happened I did not mean to stay in the valley. Too much has happened that people won't soon forget.

I told Mr. Glass that. I'm going to work for his bank, making a survey of conditions all over the Territory, arranging for cattle loans, perhaps going to Texas after new stock, trying to get the country back on its feet."

She was staring at him, white-faced.

He said, gently, "Maybe it's lucky things happened this way. It wouldn't have worked, you and I. We thought it would because we had grown up together, because we both knew what Joe John wanted and thought that was what we wanted too." He reached out and took her shoulders then and kissed her lightly on the forehead.

"Take the credit for helping the valley restock," he told her. "Keep the Box M the leader, always. Try to run things the way your father would have done. You will be far happier in the end."

She did not answer. He looked at her a long moment, then turned and went through the door, closing it quietly behind him.

"Owen, wait." It was an instinctive cry, but he did not hear it. He went on down the steps, leaving Martha Martel a little frightened, a little scared, feeling utterly alone for the first time in her selfish life.

On the street half a dozen people stopped him to ask about the happenings at Cap Rock. He answered patiently and then moved on, coming into the restaurant.

It was empty with the midafternoon lull and he walked through into the kitchen to find Mrs. Perkins peeling potatoes beside the work table.

She lifted her eyes to his face, and started to speak, and changed her mind and with a slight motion of her head indicated the door which led back into the living quarters.

He nodded and crossing knocked softly, then pushed the door open. Grace was sitting beside the stove, looking out through the side window at the snowy yard beyond. Apparently she had not heard his knock. Apparently she did not know he was in the room until he spoke, then she straightened, coming quickly to her feet.

"Owen."

He moved toward her, seeing the color rise in her cheeks, saying gently, "I've come to say goodby."

"Goodby." She was startled. "Where are you going now?"

"First to the ranch to get my things. I'll sleep there tonight, then on to Cap Rock. I'm going to work for the Land Bank."

"You're leaving the valley?" She sounded as if she could not believe it. "But the Box M . . . who will run it?"

"Martha, I suppose, with Shorty and Mac to help her."

"But you . . ."

"There's nothing for me here any more. After the trouble over the drive the other ranchers would never feel the same."

"No," she agreed. "Not the same, but the Box M was your home, this valley your life. You'll miss it, and many of us will miss you."

He said, "There are other valleys. I think I'll like the work, and it isn't far to Cap Rock. I'll come back to see you if you'll let me."

"Let you?"

"Want me to?"

Her eyes came up to meet his then and there was no reservation, no reserve, and suddenly he took three steps forward and she was in his arms, her body warm against him, her hands tightening on his shoulders as he bent to kiss her.

Afterward he stepped away, his voice shaken. "Grace, I came here to ask you to go with me and then lost my nerve. Would you, could you come to Cap Rock?"

"Anywhere," she said. "Any time." Neither of them saw Mrs. Perkins open the door and peer in, then shut it quietly, a small smile on her tired face. Neither cared. They forgot the snow and the cold and the ice storm. The world was suddenly a very wonderful place, a more wonderful place than either had ever realized existed.

Center Point Publishing
600 Brooks Road ● PO Box 1
Thorndike ME 04986-0001 USA

(207) 568-3717

US & Canada:
1 800 929-9108

LP   Ballard, Todhunter
F   Blizzard range /
BAL

DATE DUE			